Sand Letters

Book One:
Silly Love Songs
1976-1977

R. E. Bradshaw

Titles from R. E. Bradshaw Books

Rainey Bell Thriller Series:
Rainey with a Chance of Hale (2017)
Relatively Rainey (2016) Lambda Literary Awards Finalist
Carl of the Bells (2015) (Short Story-eBook only)
Colde & Rainey (2014)
The Rainey Season (2013) Lambda Literary Awards Finalist
Rainey's Christmas Miracle (2011) (Short Story-ebook only)
Rainey Nights (2011) Lambda Literary Awards Finalist
Rainey Days (2010)

The Adventures of Decky and Charlie Series:
Out on the Panhandle (2012)
Out on the Sound (2010)

Molly: House on Fire (2012)
Lambda Literary Awards Finalist

Before It Stains (2011)

Waking Up Gray (2011)

Sweet Carolina Girls (2010)

The Girl Back Home (2010)

Sand

Letters

Book One:
Silly Love Songs

1976-1977

R. E. BRADSHAW

Published by
R. E. BRADSHAW BOOKS

USA

Sand Letters
Book One: Silly Love Songs 1976-1977
By R. E. Bradshaw

© 2018 by R. E. Bradshaw. All Rights Reserved.
R. E. Bradshaw Books/January 2018
ISBN-13: 978-0-9989549-3-6

Website: http://www.rebradshawbooks.com
Facebook: https://www.facebook.com/rebradshawbooks
Twitter @rebradshawbooks
Blog: http://rebradshawbooks.blogspot.com
For information contact rebradshawbooks@gmail.com

Acknowledgments

I acknowledge the women who made and make it possible for me to sit here and write books about women who love women and get paid to do it. Thank you for believing that women's rights are human rights.

About the book…

Sometimes a book just says, "Write me." I have enjoyed meeting Margie Whooten and Ruth Ann Johnson. I am already excited for the journey that lies ahead with these two. It is my plan to follow Margie and Ruth Ann through the laughter, the tears, the complications, and the comfort of a long-standing friendship. This is book one. This is how they met. This is how a girl born in 1961 grows into one of the women wearing a pink hat and marching in 2018, carrying a sign that reads, "I can't believe I still have to protest this shit."

In the summer of the American Bicentennial, 1976, Margie Whooten is a fifteen-year-old with questions. She finds answers in a novel providence provides. Fate then throws Margie face first into the chest of her new favorite author, beginning the awakening of the young woman's soul and forming the foundation of a forever kind of friendship.

REB

Dedicated to Title IX

"No person in the United States shall, on the basis of sex, be excluded from participation in, be denied the benefits of, or be subjected to discrimination under any education program or activity receiving Federal financial assistance."

Signed into law by U.S. President Richard Nixon
June 23, 1972

"Are you talkin' to me?
Well, I'm the only one here."
—Travis Bickle
"Taxi Driver"
1976

Chapter One

July 2, 1976
"...Evert beat Goolagong to win the 83rd Wimbledon Women's Tennis Championship today. Lastly, North and South Vietnam were officially reunited after more than 20 years of war. Hanoi has been declared the capital. And that's the top of the hour news wrap up. It's eighty degrees and a bit overcast at two o'clock on this Friday afternoon. You're listening to WOBR, 1530 AM, Wanchese, N.C. Enjoy your Fourth of July weekend on the Outer Banks. Glad y'all could come on down. Now here's Hall and Oates with 'Sarah Smile.'"

On a ribbon of sand off the coast of North Carolina, atop an ancient ridge shadowed under Live Oak and Yaupon trees, a small transistor radio played from its perch in the crooked elbow of a wind-twisted branch. A lanky fifteen-year-old girl with sun-streaked hair the color of the sand she dragged a toe through, reclined in a rope hammock, one foot on the ground lazily swaying the occupant. From her relaxed vantage point, she could see the front door of her home and anyone approaching from the rear of the house. This tactical advantage was imperative because the teen didn't want her mother to see what she was reading. Cleverly disguised with an appropriated dust jacket, the novel had aroused no suspicions. However, if nosey Ida should somehow see the actual text, the fact that they were on an island might come into play. Swimming to safety would not be out of the question.

The front door screeched open. "Everything down here rusts to pieces." Ida's blonde head appeared, continuing the never-ending diatribe on her distaste for salt air and its effects. "Margie, ride your bike down to the post office and get the mail.

"Yes, ma'am."

"When you get back, would you please oil these hinges? I don't necessarily want to announce to the world every time this door opens and closes."

"Okay, momma."

Ida pushed the door back and forth a few times. With each swing, a shriek of iron on iron cut through the remains of a once thick maritime forest, as Ida Johnson Whooten ground the dry rust into the hinges and nagged a man that wasn't there.

"How could he not notice this door needs oiling? Is he deaf?" Ida noticed Margie, who was skilled at tuning her mother out, turn another page in the book. "Go on, now. You can finish that book later. Watch the traffic."

"Yes, ma'am."

Margie Whooten unwound her gangly limbs from the hammock and stood to her recently achieved growth spurt height of five-feet-eight-inches.

"Give me that book, and I'll put it in your room for you," Ida said, holding out her hand.

"It's okay, I got it."

"You have it," Ida corrected.

"I have it, thank you. I'll be back in a few."

Margie stretched her lean, muscular body, formed from being in constant motion, a state that described her entire childhood. A strong swimmer, a talented surfer, a marvel with a basketball, she wasn't often found reading quietly on a sunny summer afternoon. Although a voracious reader, that activity was reserved for nights, rainy days, and a few cold spells in winter. This wasn't an ordinary afternoon. This was the day Margie learned there were others like her. She was not alone.

On the way to the garage, as she passed the porch with the book and radio in hand, Ida called through the closed door, "It wouldn't kill you to brush your hair, maybe put in a pretty bow."

Margie did what she usually did and pretended not to hear Ida's disappointed critique of pretty much everything about her daughter. Margie's androgynous body didn't have the curves her friends were developing. Her shape was closer to Gumby than that of the Raquel Welch shapely form Ida had been hoping for. Her mother brought home training bras and then padded bras, neither of which Margie had any intention of wearing. She was probably the only flat-chested teenage girl in America who wasn't bothered by that fact. Margie figured boobs would mess with her balance on a surfboard and interfere with her shooting form. So, not having any could not have bothered her less.

Much to her mother's chagrin, Margie was unconcerned with her lagging womanliness. She had a regular period and that was about as much of womanhood as she cared to experience, particularly if the rest of it was as painfully messy. Margie had no interest in following the gaggle of girls preening for the boys down at the high school. Her lack of a "rack" and indifference didn't faze the young men who buzzed around her constantly. She could outrun most of them and not one guy her age, and very few older ones, had ever beaten her at a game of HORSE. Her superior athletic skills didn't seem to cool their enthusiasm. Margie thought she attracted the boys because, unlike her fawning female friends, she paid them no attention at all, or, and much more likely, the cause lay in the boy to girl ratio in her age group on the island. It was a female-friendly market.

Margie hooked the radio on the support she and Bob made using a coat hanger bent around the handlebars. She tied the book to the frame with an elastic cord she kept on the bike for just such needs. Bike baskets were not Margie's style. She climbed on the ten-speed she had purchased with money made from mowing lawns, which wasn't easy to do on an island with more sand than grass. Margie squeezed the hand-breaks. The aluminum rims whined against the rubber pads, as she made a controlled decent down the steep driveway and slipped out into midsummer tourist traffic, which was exceptionally heavy on this Friday before the Fourth of July. The national holiday had a special meaning this time around, as it was nineteen seventy-six, the Bicentennial of the founding of the country.

Earlier that morning, Margie returned home with her mother amid the long lines of cars filled with red, white, and blue clad tourists waving flags. The island would soon be filled to the brim with drunken sunburned patriots. The previous two days were spent in Wilson, while Margie's grandmother underwent surgery. The antsy teen endured being cooped in a hospital waiting room for hours on end. It was in this state of bored, caged-animal misery that she found the book.

Margie people-watched from her corner of the coop/waiting room, giving each a fantasy role in the spy novel playing out in her head. She was particularly interested in the reading woman by the vending machines. The woman's eyes floated over the words, her lips curling into a smile now and again. Margie soon became invested in the reading of the story from afar, so much so that she was crushed with disappointment when it ended, without having seen a word.

The woman closed the novel and held it to her breast, staring off into the distance with a grin of satisfaction. Intrigued, Margie had to know the title of this book. Fortunately, and perhaps because the woman had noticed the young voyeur, she placed the text on the table in front of her. The reading woman then gathered her things and left the waiting room. Thinking the woman may have smiled directly at her on the way out, Margie was almost positive that she winked.

After waiting five excruciating minutes, Margie had moved closer, and spent another five trying to acquire superpowers with which to read the book title on the spine from ten feet away. When the woman didn't come back, Margie closed the remaining distance and sat near the book. She could read the title, *The Belle Cracked* by Ruth Ann Johnson. Making one last check for the book owner's return, Margie picked it up and flipped it over. The blurb on the hardback novel's dust jacket said, "Following on the heels of Rita Mae Brown's *Rubyfruit Jungle*, Johnson's novel is a laugh out loud and at times heartbreaking tale of growing up lesbian in the south. Miss Johnson gives us a look into the life of Anne, a Southern Belle gone astray. Through humor and tears, the reader begins to understand how much of home one can miss, even if you live there."

Margie's eyes darted around, checking to see if anyone saw her with the novel in her hands. She put it back on the table, not like a hot potato, but slowly, as if it didn't interest her. She picked up a magazine and pretended to be absorbed in an article about the coming election, comparing President Gerald Ford, Ronald Reagan, and a peanut farmer from Georgia named Jimmy Carter. Margie remained seated, unable to leave the book and incapable of picking it up again. She scanned the other reading material on the table, formulating a plan. She saw a copy of Agatha Christie's *Sleeping Murder* with a dust cover that would suffice for camouflage. Her mother would find nothing abnormal about Margie reading another of Agatha's novels. She read insatiably, mostly because it saved her at night when she was locked inside with her parents, subject to their idea of entertainment. Mysteries were Margie's favorite, at least until now.

The picture of Ruth Ann Johnson on the back inside tab of *The Belle Cracked's* dust cover compelled Margie to keep it. She took another from the Christie book and quickly secreted her new obsession away, under the guise of Agatha's latest who-done-it. Margie thought Miss Marple would have been proud of the subterfuge.

The accompanying photograph with Ruth Ann Johnson's biography showed what Margie had heard her mother describe as a handsome woman. Margie suspected that was what was meant when a woman turned all the heads in the room, male and female. Miss Johnson wore her hair in a wavy pixie cut. It was dark, almost black hair, or that's how it appeared in the black and white photo. Her eyebrows were dark and arched over an intense gaze from nearly black eyes. Again, it could have just been the photo's gray-scale creating the illusion of Miss Johnson's obsidian stare.

Margie thought, "She doesn't look like a lesbian." Then looked around to make sure she hadn't said that aloud.

Of course, the only lesbians Margie had ever seen, to her knowledge, were the two women who came into the beauty shop over on the mainland, while she waited for her mother to get her monthly dye and set.

Margie's introduction to alternatives to the male and female bee paradigm came at eleven years old when a couple walked into Diane's House of Hair. One woman wore a dress and looked much like Margie's own mother, right down to the unfortunate platinum blonde hair color choice, another middle-income housewife living the dream. The other woman, Margie at first mistook for a man, dressed in a black suit with a white shirt and skinny black tie. Her hair slicked with pomade was worn swept back into a ducktail at the base of her neck like Fonzie on "Happy Days," except this cool guy was wearing a bra. Margie stared at both women so much her mother finally pinched her. When they got into the car to go home, Margie asked about them.

"Honey, those women are queer," Ida had said.

"They looked strange to me, too," Margie commented, thinking only that queer meant different or odd, "but why did that one dress and act like a man?"

Ida squirmed uncomfortable with the question. She gripped the steering wheel, then blurted out, "They're lesbians. Do you know what that is?'

Margie shook her head and stared wide-eyed at her mother, quite sure one of those things she had been told would be revealed when she was older was about to come to pass.

"It's when two women act like a man and a woman, like married people." Ida fumbled for a better example, "Like they love each other in *that* way."

"What way?" Margie had no idea what Ida was trying to say.

Flummoxed, all Ida could come up with was, "It just isn't right. It's a sin. Stay away from people like that."

That statement stuck with Margie. In her eleven-year-old mind, she really didn't see anything wrong with loving a girl. She loved her friend Debbie. They were inseparable. She was too young to know that her mother had more in mind than just genuinely caring for a friend. Margie and Debbie played role games all the time. Occasionally they kissed or swam holding each other, their bodies gliding through the water together. Sometimes Debbie was the boy, but mostly it was Margie's character to play. It all seemed reasonably innocent to Margie, but somehow she knew something that felt that good had to be forbidden. She knew not to let anyone else know about it, especially Ida.

Four years older and wiser, at fifteen-years-old, Margie fully understood the public's concept of lesbians, and she certainly wasn't going to tell anybody about what she and Debbie had been doing. Debbie had a boyfriend. Margie let some scrawny boy tag along with her, but a few times a year Debbie would pin Margie to a wall and kiss her. Margie lived for those kisses. It started dawning on her that she might be a lesbian, a frightening thing considering she had Ida for a mother.

The woman who left the book had winked at her, she was sure of it. Was that a knowing smile? Had the woman seen it, too? Did Margie have a red flashing sign on her forehead blinking out, "LESBIAN, LESBIAN?" When she looked in the mirror, Margie wondered how one could tell a lesbian from a *normal* girl? This was all so confusing. Margie hoped the answers were in the book she now held in her hands.

Her mother swooped into the waiting room to retrieve Margie before she could open her new treasure to the first page. She had already said goodbye to her grandmother and was more than ready to get out of the smelly hospital. Tucking the book under her arm, Margie followed Ida to the car, vibrating with the knowledge of her secret.

Even though she had her driver's permit and always begged to drive, Margie told her mother the heavy traffic made her nervous. Ida agreed it would be better if she took the wheel, leaving Margie to read the whole way home. She stretched out on the backseat of Ida's station wagon and dove into *The Belle Cracked*.

Along the way, she had to shut the book and stare at the clouds through the window to calm her breathing. Somehow, Ruth Ann Johnson had written Margie's life story. She finally quit reading when they reached the Oregon Inlet Bridge because of continued blushing she didn't want her mother to see. Margie sat up and gazed out over the ocean, its vastness representing the way she felt most of the time—alone.

As they crossed onto Hatteras Island, headed for the village of Buxton, Margie didn't feel so isolated anymore. Somebody else understood. Somebody knew the secrets she kept. To everyone, she was happy-go-lucky Margie, the athletically gifted, cute tomboy with the infectious smile. Ruth Ann knew differently. Margie loved Ruth Ann Johnson already, and she was only on Chapter Six.

#

"'It's all clear to me now,' yes it is. That was Gary Wright with 'Love Is Alive,' number ten on the Billboard charts this week. Next up, the Beatles with 'Got to Get You Into My Life.'"

#

Less than a half a mile from her home, around the lazy twenty-five-miles-per-hour curves that wound through Buxton, Margie arrived at the little white post office next to the village general store. Outside the post office, surfers crowded the tiny gravel parking lot, waiting for their turn at the window, collecting weekly checks from home so they could live the bohemian lifestyle. What a crock, Margie thought. Most of them were wealthy frat boys on summer break, trying to be hippies. The authentic hippies came and went years earlier, but Margie remembered them. The current parking lot dwellers would go back to universities in the fall, don khakis and button-down shirts, and step back into the establishment.

The real surfers were either on the beach or at work, supporting their wax habit. Margie hung out with them when she could. They would come through every season, regaling her with tales of waves on the coasts of the world, and then they would be off again, following the sun. She respected their nomad status. The frat boy surfers were not that interesting.

The crowd at the door finally dissipated enough for Margie to slip into the too small lobby. Margie squeezed her way through the coconut oil-bathed bodies toward the corner where her family's box was located. She turned the little brass dials until the combination allowed her to remove the contents. After slamming the door shut and giving the dials a locking spin, Margie pushed her way back out the entrance with her head down, trying to avoid stepping on bare toes. Instead, she ran smack into the breasts of a woman coming in the door. Margie raised her head, made eye contact with the woman, and was positive the look of surprise on her face read genuinely stunned. It simply couldn't be.

The woman smiled back at Margie, saying, "Excuse me, I'm sorry. It is rather crowded in here, isn't it?"

All Margie could manage was a weak, "Uh huh."

She darted around the woman and out the door trying to remember how to breathe. Blinking several times, unable to believe what she had just seen, Margie sat down on the wooden walkway by her bike. She pulled the book from the elastic tie, opened the fake cover, and stared at the picture on the back flap of *The Belle Cracked*'s dust jacket. It was her! That was Ruth Ann Johnson, and she was in Margie's post office. She looked back toward the door, waiting for Ruth Ann to reappear.

A young blonde sat on a hood of the car next to her, leaning back against the windshield. She startled Margie when she spoke, "That's a good book you're reading."

"Uh, yeah, I guess—I just started reading it—I found it."

Margie was horrified. Someone knew she was reading a lesbian book. There were all kinds of reasons this woman knew it was a good book, only one of which could be useful to Margie.

At just that moment, Ruth Ann Johnson walked up grinning at the blonde on the hood.

"I see you two have met. I ran into her in the post office," Ruth Ann said, indicating Margie with a nod in her direction.

"We haven't officially met, but we do have the same taste in authors." She slid off the car hood and stood in front of Margie, extending her hand. "My name is Linda."

"I'm Ma-Margie," she stuttered out, still in shock.

"Ruth Ann, I think you have a fan here," Linda said, over her shoulder to the approaching darkly handsome woman.

Margie took all of Ruth Ann in at once. The picture on the book cover did nothing to warn a person of the effect the author had in person. Ruth Ann Johnson was tall, probably five-nine or ten. She had the long, lean muscle of an athlete. Her black hair was wavy and had grown out to shoulder length since the headshot for the book cover. Her skin was tanned and glowing. Her smile filled with perfectly straight white teeth hiding behind full pink lips. With all of that approaching her, it was Ruth Ann's eyes that held Margie in a trance. They were big and deep brown with flecks of gold that seemed to twinkle in the sunlight.

Margie stumbled to her feet, sending mail scattering. The Agatha Christie book cover fluttered to the ground, but she held onto the book. Bending down to pick up the mail, she came face to face with Ruth Ann, who had stooped to help gather the strewn items.

"I see you don't plan on getting caught reading that book," she said, holding out the Christie dust cover to Margie with a knowing grin.

"Uh, well—I—" Margie couldn't form a sentence.

Ruth Ann took the book and slipped the camouflaging cover back into place. She returned it with a smile and said, "It's okay, Margie, is it?"

Margie nodded yes.

Ruth Ann went on, "When I was your age, I wouldn't have wanted anybody knowing I was reading it, much less already writing it in my head."

Margie finally regained the ability to form words. "Then it is true, isn't it?"

Ruth Ann shrugged. "Most of it. I changed names and things so I wouldn't get sued, but for the most part, it's my life."

"Mine, too." The words escaped Margie's lips before she knew she was going to say them.

Ruth Ann put a hand on Margie's shoulder and said, "Just be true to yourself. The rest will work itself out."

Linda headed for the car door, calling back to Margie, "Hey, we're staying at the Outer Banks Cottages, if you want to drop by. We're always on the deck or the beach. It was nice to meet you, Margie. Hope you enjoy the book."

Ruth Ann backed away toward the driver's side of the car. She grinned at Margie. "Yeah, come on by. We can talk about the book if you want."

And then she was gone. Margie stood there in shock. She didn't know how long she'd been staring into space when Mr. Aylett, the man who owned the general store, stuck his head out the door and asked if she was all right. She mumbled something, stuck the mail inside the book, and peddled for home.

She had just been invited to visit Ruth Ann Johnson, her new favorite author, and a real living, breathing lesbian. Her mother must never find out, but if there was a way, Margie was going to see Ruth Ann again. There was so much she wanted—no, must know. Ruth Ann would have the answers. Margie was sure of it.

Hiding the book under the back porch before going into the house, she would sneak back out to read it later, while her mother was occupied cooking supper. If she had to, Margie would tell her parents she was going flounder gigging and stay out on the sound all night reading by lantern light. She would read as fast as possible because she wanted to see Ruth Ann right away and she had to finish the book first. By morning, she would have new knowledge and a ton of questions.

She knew one thing already. There were others like her. She wasn't alone, after all.

#

"Well, that's it for us, folks. Hope you've had a great day on the Outer Banks. We'll be back with the sunrise. Dorothy Moore is going to sing you into midnight with 'Misty Blue.' Sweet dreams."

#

Margie took the little skiff out and anchored on the sandbar behind the house, where she devoured Ruth Ann Johnson's prose. Having grown up out here on the water, Margie's father trusted she would return safe and sound by morning. It wouldn't be the first time she stayed out all night fishing. Besides, she could wade to shore and barely get her hips wet. Her parents were used to Margie's Huckleberry Fin lifestyle. She made excellent grades, always at the top of her class. She stayed out of trouble, but not out of mischief. Still, she was a good girl and gave her parents no need to worry about a short summer night out on the Pamlico Sound.

Margie was where she said she'd be, but she wasn't fishing. About the time her father usually went to bed, she climbed out of the boat and walked along the sandbar with the lantern and her gig. He could see her from his second story bedroom window, and she knew he would check on her before he went to sleep. She was able to spear two nice size flounder while she waited for her father to go to bed. At least she would have evidence that she fished. She glanced up at the house several times and finally saw the master bedroom light go out. She hurried back to the boat, threw the fish on ice in the cooler, and resumed the quest to finish The Belle Cracked before dawn.

By sunrise, Margie's bleary and bloodshot eyes focused on the last page. More confident than ever that she was a lesbian, that she liked girls in *that* way, Margie closed the book knowing she was irreversibly changed. She loved Debbie, but she knew her childhood friend was just trying to be scandalous. Debbie wasn't like Margie. Ruth Ann had explained all those mixed up feelings she was having. The hint of sexual content in the book had been both uncomfortable and exhilarating. If the stirrings in her body were any indication, then yes, Margie wanted to do those things with women too. If the book agreed with Ida that merely thinking about sex with another woman could condemn Margie to hell, it would have been different. Instead, Ruth Ann had given her hope that women could love women and be happy.

Ruth Ann had chronicled her journey as the daughter of a Southern Belle who, like Ida, expected her daughter to be a dainty flower and become the wife of a doctor, attorney, or some other ostensibly secure, wealthy position. Ruth Ann rebelled. She had been a tomboy like Margie. Ruth Ann had gone along with cotillion, the debutante cycle of parties, and dated the wholesome quarterback, but she really wanted the head majorette. It had taken Ruth Ann years to come to terms with her sexuality, not managing it until sophomore year in college.

Ruth Ann had written the novel as a creative writing project senior year, according to the author's biography. It chronicled her life from birth to age twenty-two. Margie had laughed and cried, seeing herself on every page. Ruth Ann was brave and sure of herself. Margie didn't think she could be that courageous. The fear of Ida finding out the truth was enough to keep her mouth shut. Ruth Ann had kept her true feelings to herself, telling no one, not even the girl she made out with on a regular basis, the head majorette. She covered her desire for women with the obligatory boyfriend. Margie thought she'd probably have to get one of those too or people would start talking. Ruth Ann had mapped out a plan for Margie. She'd get through high school playing the game, get off this island, go to college, and never look back.

#

"The Fourth of July 1976, the two-hundredth birthday of the U.S.A., and in the number one position on this Independence Day is an artist from the Mother Country, the country we rebelled against two centuries ago to gain our independence. That's what the holiday and the celebration are all about. Well, on America's record charts Britannia rules again. Here's that very popular Englishman Paul McCartney with his group Wings and the number one song in the colonies on this July 4, 1976, 'Silly Love Songs'...I'm Casey Kasem. Join me next week and again we'll count down the forty most popular songs in the USA. Until then, keep your feet on the ground and keep reaching for the stars."
—American Top 40, Broadcast Saturday, July 3, 1976

#

Just after noon, following a much-needed nap, Margie asked her dad for a ride to Lighthouse Road. She promised to be home by dark. By now, her parents pretty much let her do as she pleased during the day. She surfed most of the time or worked out at the gym. Her father, Bob Whooten, taught math and was the boys basketball and baseball coach.

Margie lived in the gym in the cold months and on the beach in the warm ones. They could find her if they wanted to. She always went where she said she was going, but not today.

As soon as her father was out of sight, she tucked the surfboard under her arm and made her way up Highway Twelve, toward the Outer Banks Cottages at the north edge of Buxton village. Margie knew the people who ran the motel. Down on the island, everybody knew everybody. She didn't want to be seen with Ruth Ann, just in case anybody else knew she was an author, a lesbian one. The phone lines would physically burn down to Ida, and she would come to wrangle her wayward daughter with the station wagon tires smoking. Margie had to be careful.

Ida Johnson Whooten said she "came from people." In the south, that meant her family had a colonial heritage and centuries tied to the land, Daughters of the American Revolution and all that. They owned slaves too, which Ida tried to dismiss as just the way it was. At one time Ida's people had money, old money. The Civil War took most of their wealth, but not their manners or their pretentious airs. Ida was raised with more pride than money. She intended her daughter to do better. They were middle class through and through, but Ida maintained the illusion of status she believed due her bloodlines. Her daughter would be the "Belle of the Ball." The money would come back one day, Ida was sure of it. She invested those hopes in Margie.

To her mother's consternation, Margie had not played along. Frilly undergarments were found discarded in the yard. Patent leather shoes were not made for climbing trees, and foot coverings, in general, were to be worn only when absolutely necessary. Dresses were for girls who chased boys. Margie let the boys try to catch her, but they couldn't. She wasn't a cheerleader. Margie rather liked the cheers being for her, as she tore down the basketball court, wowing the crowd with her ball handling and dead-eye jump shot. The only debut Margie was ever going to make was as a shooting guard for a top-ranked college team. Yet, Ida kept trying.

When in public, Ida gave the appearance of pure southern ladyship. Everyone loved her. She was the life of the party. Margie, however, lived with Ida and it was no party. Her mother spent the majority of the time she was near her daughter criticizing the way Margie wore her hair, her clothes choices, the fact that she preferred playing ball to almost anything else. She nitpicked at Margie and Bob until they both spent as much time out of her presence as possible. Ida claimed it was not carping; it was her way of trying to improve the two of them. What she didn't realize was that Bob and Margie liked themselves the way they were. There was no doubt in Margie's mind that her mother loved both of them, but sometimes she thought her mother was going to love them to death.

Margie didn't have to imagine what Ida's reaction would be to Ruth Ann Johnson. Her mother would make an island rocking scene, then lock Margie in the house and berate her for hours. If Margie had heard the speech about reputation once, she'd heard it a million times.

Her mother would start, "If you lie down with dogs, you get fleas. All you have in this life is your reputation. You only get one. You muck that up, and you might as well go on and marry the first thing that comes along, because no decent man will have you, blah, blah, blah..."

That's how it always started. Then Ida would relay stories of good girls gone bad and sullied reputations until Margie's eyes would roll up in her head. Bob was no help. He would hide, wait for the storm to pass because he feared that somehow the focus would turn to him. Locked in the house, Margie would endure hours of "constructive criticism." Eventually, her mother would grow tired of Margie underfoot, bouncing a ball or playing music too loud, and subsequently free her from bondage.

Fully aware of all the reasons she shouldn't, Margie cut off the highway and made her way to the beach. She trudged through the sand at a good pace, until she saw Ruth Ann and Linda in the distance. They were laughing, sitting in beach chairs under an umbrella, Budweiser cans poking out of little handheld Styrofoam coolers.

Margie slowed down. She didn't want to appear too eager or breathless. Lugging her surfboard a half a mile in ninety-degree heat hadn't been easy. She dropped her tee shirt and shorts on the beach, revealing an orange and blue flowered bikini. Margie envied the boys' shorts. One good wipeout, and that bikini could disappear never to be seen again. She double checked the square knots she tied to be sure it stayed in place, though she didn't plan on getting thrown in the spin cycle on a calm day like today.

After fastening the board leash to her ankle, Margie walked down to the water and threw herself into the breakers. She paddled to where a few other surfers were waiting for the next set. Margie didn't know them. From the looks of the new boards, these guys were amateurs. Margie was not. Her parents' rule was she could never surf without other surfers present. Noting this bunch could be more hazardous than the waves, she kept her distance. Margie had been at home in the sea from the first time her father dangled her feet in the salt water. She would take the ocean lifeguard test in August. Margie already knew she could pass it. The test was part of a workout regime her father developed for her. Still, the beaches of the Diamond Shoals were no place to tread alone.

Margie had been standing on a surfboard solo since the age of five and might have been earlier if not for Ida's objections. The thrill of riding waves had seized her on the first set. She wanted to compete on legendary breaks, but had to be content with the little island curl. Ida put her foot down and squashed the world traveling surfer girl dream to bits. There was no use even thinking about it. The only reason Ida hadn't been able to stop her from playing basketball was Bob. He saved Margie from a life of tiaras and beauty pageants at an early age. The coach in him recognized Margie's raw athletic talent and nurtured her into the player she was destined to be. He won the argument with Ida by guaranteeing Margie would go to the best colleges available based on her athletic talent alone, not to mention her academics.

Sitting up on the board, her legs dangling below, Margie peered into the horizon. Offshore, three waves were building back to back. Margie knew the eager amateurs would duck-in if she took the first two, so she set her eyes on the third. As predicted, the first wave caught the fancy of two of the guys; the second wave took the rest. She lay down, paddled into position, and popped up to her feet as soon as the sea's power took her board. Margie carved across the smooth face of the wave, going to the top and cutting back down. For a few precious seconds of surfing bliss she skated on the glassy surface inside the closing curl, and then rode the white foam as far as it would take her toward shore.

Hopping off the board with practiced skill, Margie tucked it under her arm and approached the shore. She headed back down the beach where her shirt and shorts had been cast off. Riding the wave in the direction she did, Margie made it possible to walk nonchalantly in front of Ruth Ann and Linda, or at least she hoped it appeared innocent enough.

"Very nice," Ruth Ann called out. "Can you teach me how to do that?"

Margie walked over to the umbrella, still dragging the board leash and dripping wet. "How much time do you have?"

"Here, sit down," Ruth Ann indicated the blanket on the ground.

Margie accepted the invitation with a dry-throated, "Thank you."

"I'll be here another week. Could I learn that fast?" Ruth Ann asked.

Linda chuckled, "You'll probably break your neck."

Excited at the prospect of spending more time with Ruth Ann, Margie surprised herself, blurting out, "You look athletic enough. If you spent every day working on it, I don't see why I couldn't at least get you standing up."

Margie suddenly longed for a pair of sunglasses. Ruth Ann was wearing a white bikini. There wasn't an ounce of fat on her body. Her hip bones stuck out enough to hold the waist of her suit bottom away from her skin. A thin line of soft dark hair trailed down from her belly button and disappeared below the material. Margie tried desperately not to look, but her eyes kept being drawn over the length of Ruth Ann's body and she was sure both women knew it. Margie began fumbling with the board leash on her ankle to cover all of what was happening inside her head and body.

"I could pay you," Ruth Ann said, continuing the conversation.

"No, that's not necessary," Margie said from behind her knee, still hiding from the natural force of attraction radiating from Ruth Ann Johnson.

"Are you sure? I'd really like to learn."

The initial overawed feelings of the moment began to wane, allowing Margie to regain her composure. She hoped she had done so without ever letting on how incredibly confused but absolutely alive she felt. It took a bit, but Margie finally made eye contact with the smiling Ruth Ann. That smile and those eyes were intoxicating. Margie knew she could deny this woman nothing, even if she had no idea what all that entailed.

Margie grinned and answered, "We can start Monday morning if you'd like. About nine?"

"That sounds like a plan. Thank you, Margie. I look forward to our lessons." Ruth Ann extended her hand for Margie to shake.

Margie shook it and added, "It should be lots of fun."

Linda, who Margie had almost forgotten was there, spoke up, "So, did you finish the book?"

Margie blushed. "Yes, I finished it this morning."

Linda cocked her head and looked Margie over good. "May I ask how old you are?"

Margie was embarrassed to be so young. She answered meekly, "I turned fifteen last Friday."

Linda was kind. She reached out and patted Margie on the knee. "So, this is all just starting for you isn't it?"

Margie felt as if she could tell these women anything, which was unusual after years of hiding most of what she thought. Maybe it was because someone understood how she felt for the first time. Whatever the reason, Margie was comfortable enough to say, "I didn't even know what this was until I read that book."

Ruth Ann and Linda both laughed, not at her, but with her, because Margie started laughing, too.

"I had a sneaking suspicion that I felt differently about things than my friends," Margie said, "but I wasn't sure until now."

Ruth Ann stopped laughing and asked, "Are you okay with it? I mean, you don't seem traumatized."

Margie paused a second before she replied, "I think I'm okay with being me. I'm just so glad I'm not the only one." The older women smiled at each other and then at her. Margie assumed they had experienced the same elation at discovering other women like themselves. She went on, "I think I'm going to have to play the game to get out of here, though. You know what I mean?"

Ruth Ann slapped her thigh, laughing. "I know exactly what you mean."

Margie said, "Yeah, I guess you do. I just read all about it."

Linda said, "Tell us about you, Margie. All I know is your name, that you surf better than most of the men out here, and you do it with incredible grace."

Ruth Ann sat up on the edge of her chair, resting her elbows on her knees and clasping her hands in front of her. Her new favorite author was interested in what Margie had to say, and that set parts of her young body on fire again. The golden flecks in Ruth Ann's eyes winked and tugged at some place deep in Margie's gut. She dug her toes into the sand and tore herself away from the older woman's gaze.

Ruth Ann encouraged her, "Come on, I know there's a story there."

Margie caved, immediately spilling her life story to these complete strangers. "I was born in Wilson County, where my parents are from. I'm an only child. We moved here when I was two. My dad is the basketball and baseball coach at the school. We have only one, and it's K-12. I've gone to school with the same people in the same building for going on my tenth year. I make straight A's. I play point guard on the basketball team. My dad says I'm good enough to get a scholarship, which I intend to take and run as far away from here as I can."

Ruth Ann smiled at Margie. "Don't try to get too far from your roots. They are what made you who you are. I'm not saying don't go explore that big world out there, just remember where you came from. It'll bring you comfort on a cold night."

Linda added, "When you do finally come out, some of these people will treat you differently, but not as many as you might think. Too many times we don't see how we approach people after we announce we're lesbians. We often get the reaction we anticipate. I'm just wondering how much of that is due to the expectation of disgust."

"Oh, I'm not going to be announcing anything to anybody. I know how my mother is going to react. I don't have any doubts about that," Margie said, digging her feet deeper into the sand.

Ruth Ann asked, "Anything like the book?"

Margie grinned at her. "Yep, though I doubt it was as funny living through it."

Ruth Ann sat back, a flash of darkness washed across her face before she smiled and said, "You're very wise for fifteen, Margie."

"You learn how to survive living with Ida."

Linda asked, "Is that your mother?"

"Yes, and she's bound and determined I'm going to be a sorority girl and marry a rich doctor. I'd rather be the rich doctor and marry the sorority girl."

Ruth Ann laughed loudly. "Margie, you are going to be a force to be reckoned with. Keep the faith, my child, keep the faith."

"God, I wish I had that much confidence at fifteen," Linda added.

Margie wondered about the two women's relationship. "May I ask you a question?"

"Sure," Ruth Ann sat up again, giving Margie her full attention, which was almost too much. It made Margie lightheaded.

She finally stuttered out. "Are you two—uh—dating?"

Ruth Ann exchanged a smile with Linda. "Yes, we've been dating for a year now. We don't live together. We live in different places."

"I live in Chicago. I work as a TV news reporter there. I come down to Chapel Hill whenever I can, and we plan vacations together," Linda added.

"I live in Chapel Hill, but I've been traveling a lot this last year with the book tour. I start graduate school and a full-time faculty job in the fall."

Margie asked, "What are you going to teach?"

Ruth Ann brightened. It was obvious she was excited about her future. "Well, the book got me in the door of the new Women's Studies department. I'll teach one class on the new voice of women in literature, concentrating on the feminist movement."

"That sounds fascinating," Margie said. "I had no idea a whole department was set aside to study women. I should look into that."

Linda asked, "Is that what you want to study when you go to college?"

"Women? Maybe, I don't know. I used to think I wanted to be a coach like my dad, but I just can't see myself teaching high school. I'm on the school newspaper staff, and I like that. I'll be the lead sports reporter next year."

Linda grew more excited, "Margie, you're at just the right age. Women are breaking into the sports reporting field."

Ruth Ann interjected, "You still have time to make up your mind."

"Yes, but it's so exciting for her," Linda said enthusiastically. "Things are changing for women in leaps and bounds. Margie has opportunities we only dreamed of at her age."

"How old are you?" Margie asked.

"Ruth Ann is twenty-six, and I'm thirty."

"That's not so old. Couldn't you pursue those same opportunities?" Margie didn't see what the big deal was. The whole feminist movement escaped her. She'd never been told she couldn't do something because she was a girl. She was better than most of the boys at boy things anyway.

Linda smiled at her the way adults sometimes did. It said to Margie, *"Oh, sweet innocent thing, you'll know the reason someday."* Another load of crap. Margie saw no reason for gender to interfere with her goals. It never occurred to her that someone would tell her no. Even if they did, she'd do it anyway.

Ruth Ann answered her question; "Doors are open for you now that were closed to us. You don't know the impact of what's happening around you in the women's movement and for homosexuals. You should educate yourself. I know that's hard for you to do here on this isolated island. Go to the library as much as you can. Read the newspapers, lots of newspapers, from all over. You'll miss out on opportunities if you don't. But that said, I admire your attitude. You just keep thinking there aren't any doors, and maybe the barriers won't be there when you arrive."

Linda said, "It was only three years ago when the American Psychiatric Association removed homosexuality from its official list of mental diseases. It's still illegal in many states, but things are changing. You don't remember a world without Title IX. Do you know what that is?"

"My dad said it meant if they offered a boys program they had to offer the same or equal program for girls, not just in sports, but any program offered by the school."

"That's right," Linda said, "and we didn't have that. Many educational programs prohibited women. There were very few organized team sports for girls. That was just four years ago, and now they're talking about professional women's basketball. Margie, the world is opening up for women your age. Your generation is going to change the way women are perceived."

"I hope we do a good job," Margie said, playing in the sand with her toes.

"If they are all like you, it should be interesting to watch," Ruth Ann said, followed by a burst of laughter.

Linda looked at her watch. "Honey, you have to go make that phone call to your editor."

Linda stood up and started gathering throws and towels. Ruth Ann and Margie rose and stepped off the blanket.

Ruth Ann extended her hand, "It was good to see you again, Margie. I look forward to our lessons."

Margie shook her hand, "Me too. Can you meet me at the lighthouse? The swell's better there."

"Nine o'clock, Monday morning. I'll be there."

Margie picked up the surfboard and walked back down the beach. She often gave lessons to kids at the lighthouse for extra cash. Some parent would pay her to babysit little Johnny or Jill, spending the morning teaching them to ride the small swell. Margie's parents knew this and would not think twice about another round of lessons. She just wouldn't tell them who the student was. The rest of this week was going to be fantastic.

Margie looked back over her shoulder at where the two women had been. She saw them walking toward the motel. Ruth Ann turned to look in Margie's direction and waved. Margie felt the tug in her gut again and waved. In less than twenty-four hours, Margie discovered a book that explained her feelings, met the author, and had now developed a giant crush on her. Margie was a lesbian, no doubt about it. Ida was going to blow a gasket if she found out. Keeping her from discovering this secret for the next three years was going to be a nightmare.

#

"Good morning. It's 6:00 a.m. on the two-hundredth birthday of this great country of ours. It's going to be an overcast day, but still warm and in the low eighties. A few showers are expected in the early evening. All in all it should be a Happy Bicentennial on the Outer Banks. Let's get you moving this morning with Captain & Tennille. My momma told me, you better 'Shop Around.'"

#

President Gerald Ford presided over the nationally televised Washington, D. C., fireworks display on the Fourth of July. While the sky over the Potomac exploded in a blaze of celebratory glory, the Whooten family and their neighbors were not seated in front of a television set celebrating Independence Day. As had been their practice all of Margie's life, the family loaded up the coolers and pulled the fishing dory down to the beach at first light. Friends gathered to repair and stretch Bob Whooten's seldom used hobby nets.

Margie's father didn't fish for a living, but many of his students' families did. This boat and the nets it carried into the sea bonded Bob with the community of men with whose sons he spent the majority of his time. More time and sometimes fatherly affection, he told Margie, than those men with hard callused hands had left to give at the end of a long fisherman's day. On the Fourth, no one fished for a living. Today, they set the nets for a huge fish fry on the beach. On the south side of Cape Hatteras point, Margie's friends and family celebrated America's birthday the island communal way.

Margie surfed for a couple of hours after the net was set and then ate from the bounty of pot-luck laden Tupperware and sampled a bit of grilled everything. She climbed into the back of her father's WWII Dodge WC54 surplus ambulance for a nap. The "Power Wagon" as her family called it, had cots in the back with what Margie speculated could have been blood. Her father assured her the vehicle never left the states, but still Margie's imagination ran to the dramatic.

Not surprisingly, Margie dreamed of Ruth Ann, or more specifically the debutante protagonist in *The Belle Cracked*. Only it was Ida chasing the young woman across the roof of Howard Johnson's, vowing to send her to Dix Hospital for electroshock therapy. Suddenly, Margie was the one being chased by a straightjacket wielding Ida. She forced herself awake when dream-Ida grabbed dream-Margie's foot as she tried to crawl away. Margie sprang into a sitting position so fast she slammed her forehead into the railing of the cot above.

"Hey, that was some dream," Debbie said.

Margie panted, the panic having not fully receded.

"Are you okay?" Debbie asked, stepping up into the back of the ambulance. She sat next to Margie on the cot. "Sorry, we're late. Jerry had a big haul this morning. I had to wait for him to come back from the docks and pick me up."

Debbie paused, waiting for a comment. When none came, she said, "Margie, talk to me."

"Just let me wake up, will ya'?" Margie didn't want to tell Debbie about the dream. She rubbed the knot on her forehead and said, "Damn, that hurt."

"Sorry. Hey, your mom sent me to find you. Jerry is going to take us to your house to get another cooler to put ice in."

"I don't want to ride around with your boyfriend," Margie said, still rubbing her head.

"Don't be like that, Margie. Jerry is a nice guy and he has a truck. He has a boat full of crab pots his grandpa lets him work. He's going to be a junior, and he's already making money."

"Wow, he's all set. When's the ceremony?" Margie didn't wait for an answer and moved around Debbie to exit out the back of the ambulance.

"Geeze, Margie. You're in a foul mood."

Margie walked down to the surf and waded in. Debbie followed. Margie had cleared her head with a dive under a few big swells.

When they were a good distance from everyone else, Debbie said, "So, I haven't seen you since you left to see your grandmother at the hospital. You didn't call when you got back and then you were gone yesterday when I called. What's up, Margie? Are you mad because I spend so much time with Jerry?"

"I don't think you should lie to the guy. That's all," Margie said, emboldened by her new knowledge.

"Lie to him? About what?"

"Debbie, you know what. You're lying to yourself too."

"Please, Margie. Stop talking in riddles. What in the hell is wrong with you?"

"There isn't anything wrong with me. I'm a lesbian, that's all. I'm not afraid to admit it. How about you?"

Debbie froze for a second, the two friends floated up and down with the swells in the calm chest deep water. Margie didn't know what Debbie was thinking in that exact moment. Margie, however, became focused on Debbie's ample bosom bobbing in the swells. The moment was fleeting.

Debbie started laughing. "Good one, Margie." She let go more trills of laughter, before saying, "Man, you had me going."

"I'm not kidding, Debbie. We're lesbians. We like to kiss each other."

"Shut the hell up, Margie. That doesn't make us lesbians, for Christ sake. My sister said all girls play with each other. It's how we prepare for the boys."

"Are you telling me you don't feel anything when you kiss me?"

Debbie backed away from Margie. "No, Margie, not like that. You're wrong. You'll see. The right guy will come along and you'll understand."

Margie smirked at Debbie. "Yeah, well, the next time you need to be kissed properly, give me a call."

"Margie, what's happened to you?"

"Nothing, yet, but I think it's going to."

"Margie Whooten, you are insane. We're going to get ice. Are you coming?"

Margie followed her best friend out of the surf. When she caught up to Debbie, she said, "I'm not insane. I'm a feminist now."

"Oh, that explains a lot."

#

"Good morning, Outer Banks. It's clear out there right now at 9:00 a. m. and already 78 degrees, but we're expecting overcast afternoon skies and thunderstorms late tonight. Join us tomorrow morning at 10:00 for American Top 40, where I hear this song is making a run for the number one spot. Here's the Manhattans with 'Kiss and Say Goodbye.'"

#

The following Friday morning, Margie ate breakfast quickly and finished her chores. There were no free rides at Ida's house. She was extremely helpful to her mother, not even complaining about having to clean the toilets this time. Margie cajoled Ida into giving her a ride to the lighthouse at eight thirty.

She had been the perfect daughter all week, running off to the beach each morning for surfing lessons. Returning in the afternoons and escaping to the air conditioned school library in the heat of the day, where her mother thought it was nice that she was interested in studying during the summer months. After supper, she worked out in the gym for two hours and returned to the house too tired to fight sleep.

Every day, while Ruth Ann learned to surf, they talked about what Margie was discovering during her afternoon reading excursions. To Margie, Ruth Ann was a wise old sage at twenty-six. She had seen so much. Ruth Ann had been in the front row, observing, writing about the feminist movement since she graduated from college. She was a fountain of knowledge to an isolated island girl, not to mention she was beautiful.

Margie told Ruth Ann about Debbie and how she still kissed her occasionally, but not so much now that she had a boyfriend. For the first time in her life, Margie had someone to talk to that would not judge her. Ruth Ann listened and commented occasionally, but mostly she let Margie talk. She understood what Margie was going through and encouraged her to relax.

Ruth Ann patted Margie's shoulder after yesterday's lesson. "The answers you are looking for will come in time. I know you want to understand everything all at once, but trust me, patience really is a virtue."

This would be their last day together. Margie had to go with her mother tomorrow to her grandmother's. Every time she thought about never seeing Ruth Ann again, Margie's stomach turned over with nausea. She tried not to think about it, concentrating on the waves with an occasional glance over her shoulder to look for Ruth Ann. She dug her toes in the sand and hugged her knees to her chest. The only person she could talk to was leaving.

Margie glanced back at the lighthouse in time to see Ruth Ann bound over the barrier dune carrying a new surfboard under her arm. Margie helped Ruth Ann pick it out the day before, after their lesson. They were going to go out together today. Up to now, Ruth Ann had used Margie's board, but today they would surf side by side. It was the closest thing to physically bonding with Ruth Ann that she could do, because this was Margie's sanctuary and the shared experience of riding a wave was soul deep.

Linda didn't come today. She had several times before, but stayed on shore reading. Margie had Ruth Ann alone for four hours every morning for the past four days. It had been the most magical sixteen hours of Margie's life to this point. She wasn't sure if anything would ever top it. When she wasn't with Ruth Ann she was thinking about her. Her departure was going to crush Margie and she knew it, but she was bound and determined not to spend their last four hours together pouting. She smiled at the approaching Ruth Ann and bit her lip to control the pain that was already starting.

"I can't wait to try out this board. I took it out at the motel yesterday afternoon, but there were no good waves," Ruth Ann said, as she approached.

"Nah, it was flat yesterday afternoon. Looks good this morning though." Margie said this while still staring out at the waves, because she couldn't look at Ruth Ann. No matter how hard she tried to delay it, the consuming ache had begun. Ruth Ann must have noticed all wasn't well.

"Hey, are you okay?"

"Yeah," Margie said, but she wasn't. A tear betrayed her as it trickled down her face. She broke. "What am I going to do now? You're the only person I can talk to."

Ruth Ann dropped the surfboard in the sand and sat down beside Margie, putting an arm around her shoulder. They sat quietly for a moment, before Ruth Ann spoke. "You're not alone, Margie. We'll keep in touch. You can write to me. I'll write you back."

Margie was into a full-on crying jag now. She gasped for air, before saying, "You can't! My mother would see your name on the envelope and freak out."

"Look, we'll figure out something. If I send you a letter from school you could just tell her it's a recruiting letter."

"Oh, she'd demand to see that, believe me." Margie saw no way around Ida.

"I'll get in touch with you and she won't know who I am, trust me, okay. I think I'd like to keep up with you, Margie. I want to know what you end up becoming. I'd like to keep you as a friend."

Margie brightened. "I'd like to be your friend, too. Will I ever see you again?"

Ruth Ann smiled, "Yes, you will. I just booked the same two weeks next summer at the motel, so I'll be back."

Margie's heart leapt for joy. A year was a long time, but she could wait. Ruth Ann was coming back. The clouds over her heart parted and the sun began to shine. Margie quit crying immediately. Ruth Ann noticed and grinned at her. She gave Margie a squeeze and a sweet little kiss on her forehead.

"No, Margie Whooten, I don't want to miss watching you grow up."

Margie followed Ruth Ann down to the water's edge, fairly floating over the sand. The spot where Ruth Ann had kissed her forehead still burned. Margie thought it would still be burning next year when Ruth Ann came back. They surfed together, laughing and splashing, enjoying each other's company. When it came time to part, Margie followed Ruth Ann to the lighthouse parking lot. She hugged her new best friend so tightly, Ruth Ann grunted.

"You take care of yourself, Margie."

Crocodile tears rolled down Margie's cheeks. She let go of Ruth Ann and backed up a couple of steps. Holding Ruth Ann had not made the parting easier. Neither of them had on more than a bikini. Their skin touching sent a thrill through Margie she'd never experienced, even though her heart was breaking.

She finally managed to whisper, "I'll see you next year."

Margie turned and walked back to the beach, leaving Ruth Ann in the parking lot. She didn't look back. She couldn't. She was afraid her heart would actually break right in two if she did. The pain was excruciating. It clasped her chest and wouldn't let her get a full breath. She paddled out into the water and let the salt from her tears blend with the ocean, where she stayed until she had no more tears left to give. It was going to be a long year.

#

"It's coming up on 8:00 p.m. It's 78 degrees and still drizzling over the Outer Banks. Let's get started with the weekly Billboard top twenty with Queen and 'You're My Best Friend.'"

#

Margie moped all weekend. Her mother commented several times, but for the most part seemed to pass it off as teenage moodiness. When they arrived home Sunday evening, a particularly sullen Margie stomped into the house ahead of her mother, carrying only her little suitcase. She left her mother to fend for herself. Ida's protestations fell on deaf ears. Her father was sitting in his customary position in the La-Z-Boy rocker watching TV when Margie blew through the den.

He called after her, "There's a package on the kitchen table for you. It was delivered to the Outer Banks Cottages because the sender didn't know your address. They called and I picked it up."

Margie ran to the kitchen. She grabbed the package and flew up the stairs to her room. Her father called after her. "Who's it from?"

Margie yelled back, already ripping the brown paper wrapper, "The lady I taught how to surf."

His "Oh," followed her into her room, but the closing of her bedroom door cut off any further communication.

Margie's heart was beating so fast she could hear the blood rushing by her eardrums. She dropped her suitcase on the floor and put the package on the bed. She sat down, took a deep breath, and pulled off the rest of the brown paper. An elegant powder blue pattern over a white background covered the top of a box. Highlights of gold here and there in the hoops and swirls on the lid glinted in the light from her bedside lamp. She ran her fingers over the raised pattern.

"It's beautiful," she whispered.

Margie slowly slid the lid off the box. Inside, tied with a blue satin ribbon lay the most beautiful writing paper she had ever seen. On one side of the box was a compartment for the matching envelopes, also tied with a satin ribbon. Above the paper, a slip of ribbon attached to the lid on another thinner compartment begged Margie to pull it. She did, revealing a sleek, black, Montblanc pen. She lifted the pen out of the box and stared at it. Margie knew these pens cost a bundle. She always looked at them in the jewelry store at the mall in Wilson.

She jumped, nearly sending the box to the floor, when her mother knocked on the door. "Margie, are you hungry?"

She was, but she said, "No, I think I'm just going to bed."

Margie quickly hid the package and the wrapping paper under the bed and went to the door. Her mother would barge in any second, because she had now waited what she deemed the appropriate amount of time to give Margie what Ida called privacy. To Margie that meant after the knock she had seconds to prepare for her mother's entry. Years of practice had made her good at it.

She opened the door and leaned on the door jam, stretching her arm across the opening, thus preventing Ida's entry into her room. Her mother could sniff out deceit like a foxhound. Margie tried to be sleepy and bored.

"Your daddy said you got a gift from the lady you taught to surf this week. I thought you were teaching a kid."

"No, it was a lady," Margie yawned and stretched.

"What did you get?" Ida tried to enter, but Margie's extended stretch prevented her from getting through.

"Oh, just some stationary and a pen. It was nice. Boy, I'm tired."

"Well, that was nice. You be sure to write her a thank you note."

Margie kissed her much shorter mother on the cheek. "I will. Good night, Mom." She called down the stairs, "Good night, Dad."

She heard him say, "Good night, honey."

Ida kissed Margie's cheek and said, "Good night, darling. I hope you are in a better mood tomorrow."

Margie shut the door and ran back to the bed. She slid on her knees and yanked the box out from its hiding place. She turned around, leaning against the bed, and put the box on her lap. When she opened the lid this time she noticed a loose envelope under the others with her name on it. She took out the enclosed letter, and read.

> *Dear Margie,*
>
> *I told you I would figure out a way for us to write. On the bottom of this note is the number and combination to your very own Post Office box. I talked to the lady there. She knows you and your mother. She laughed and said she'd be happy to keep your secret. I'll have to meet this Ida one day. She sounds very much like my mother.*
>
> *I'm enclosing my address in Chapel Hill. Linda's is there, too. She said you could write her if you have questions about*

your journalism career. I say keep your options open. There's no telling what you'll do.

So, until we meet again, write and let me know how things are going. Thank you for the surfing lessons. Keep reading and start writing. I know you've got a story to tell. Remember, Margie, just be true to yourself. You've got plenty of time to figure out the rest of this crazy world.

See you next summer.
Your friend,
Ruth Ann
P. S. Look under the paper.

Margie lifted the paper and looked in the bottom of the box. A compartment for holding things one might need in correspondence was just large enough to contain two paperbacks side by side. She sat the paper on the floor and pulled out the books. The first was a copy of Ruth Ann's novel. Margie opened it and saw that Ruth Ann had signed it, *"To my surfing coach. Thank you, Margie. Your friend, Ruth Ann"* The second book was *Rubyfruit Jungle*, by Rita Mae Brown. Ruth Ann had said it was one of her favorite books. She opened the front cover. The inscription read, *"Margie, I thought you should have this for your collection. Ruth Ann."* Under Ruth Ann's signature was another inscription. *"To Ruth Ann, Best Wishes, Rita Mae."* Ruth Ann had given Margie her autographed copy.

#

July 12, 1976

Dear Ruth Ann,

Thank you so much for the stationary and pen. The Post Office box was a stroke of genius. Only someone who grew up with a mother like Ida could understand what it's like. Thank you. Thank you.

Also, thank you for the books. I will treasure them always. I'm almost finished with Rita Mae's book. She's nearly as funny as you are. I can see why you liked it. I can't believe you gave me your autographed copy. I will take good care of it. I have a hidey-hole in my room, so Mom won't find it.

I guess I just wanted to say I received the package and thank you. I look forward to writing more, but I have to go finish "Rubyfruit Jungle." Thank you, again.
   Your friend,
   Margie

#

"Now, before we hear the one most popular song in America this week on American Top 40, let's see what's at the top of the other charts. On the soul chart the number one song is 'Something He Can Feel' – Aretha Franklin. Number one on the country chart is 'Teddy Bear' by Red Sovine. The number one best selling album again this week is Wings At The Speed of Sound. And on Billboard's national singles chart the best selling song in the U. S. A. for the second week in a row, The Starland Vocal Band with 'Afternoon Delight.'"
—*American Top 40, Broadcast July 17, 1976*

#

July 18, 1976

Dear Margie,
I was delighted to find your letter in the post a few days ago. Am just now able to sit down and jot you a few lines. I have been moving into a new house since returning and haven't had much time for anything other than packing and unpacking.
You are very welcome for the stationary and the pen. I hope you will put the pen to good use and write down everything. I think you could be a great writer. I hear it in the way you tell your tales. You are a natural storyteller.
I'll be heading to the Michigan Womyn's Music Festival the first week in August. It's the first music festival just for women. I'm going to be covering the story for several magazines. I wish you could come. I'm sure it would blow you away. I'm sure it will blow me away, as well. I'll write and tell you all about it when I get back. Hang ten.
   Your friend,
   Ruth Ann
   P.S. Glad you liked Rita Mae.

#

The Montreal Summer Olympics are held July 17-August 1, 1976. Women's Basketball makes its Olympic debut under Head Coach Billie Jean Moore and Assistant Coach Sue Gunter. Lusia Harris of Delta State scores the first basket, and the team wins the Silver in the round-robin competition. Nancy Lieberman is the youngest of the women's basketball players at eighteen. The team was co-captained by a twenty-four-year-old forward out of Tennessee-Martin, who is also in her second year as head coach for the University of Tennessee, Pat Head.

#

July 23, 1976

Dear Ruth Ann,

I finished reading "Rubyfruit Jungle." I guess what I got from it was to just try to be myself and see what happens. Kind of the same thing I got from your book. It's just nice to know I'm not crazy. I was beginning to wonder. Looks like you turned out all right.

The waves were good today. I spent all day down at the lighthouse. There were lots of guys from all over the world, down this week. I even met some girls that travel together in a van. They just go where they want and work until they have enough money to go again. That sure sounds like the life; just surfing and traveling. Ida would kill me, but maybe she couldn't find me. It's something to think about anyway.

I go to the library a lot. Miss Loris helps me find good books to read, only she really likes the Bronte sisters and I think they're a little depressing. Can you suggest some good books? I've read a bunch of old books, but not too many new ones. Our library is small, but she said she'd order books for me from the big library on the mainland. She gets more newspapers from all over now that she knows someone is actually reading them. I got the reading list for English class this year. Yuck! More Bronte, but at least "The Outsiders" is on there. I loved that book. Have you read it?

Hope the festival was fun. I don't know any feminist singers. Can you name some of them, so I can look them up?

Your friend,

Margie

#

On August 14, 1976, 10,000 Northern Ireland women demonstrate for peace in Belfast. "Don't Go Breaking My Heart" by Elton John and Kiki Dee is the number one song in America.

#

August 14, 1976

Dear Margie,

Just got back in town and catching up on all the piled up mail. The Michigan Womyn's Music Festival article is written and off to the publishers. I had a wonderful time, but I must admit I do like my warm shower here at home. The organizers were expecting only a thousand women, but over two thousand showed up. They had to truck in water, because this was out in the woods. The stage was a little wooden deck about a foot off the ground. Let me just say it was primitive, but the music and the feeling of belonging made up for any bad things. Men tried to come on "the land," as the organizers called it. Some of the things the men said, as they drove around and looked on from the tops of trees, I really can't repeat. You should know there are people like that out there.

Holly Near, Meg Christianson, Ginny Clemmons, and Cris Williamson are just some of the artists who performed. They sat right out in the audience with everyone else, listening to other performers. I camped next to Ginny Clemmons. She's a folk singer. Very nice and charming. The music was worth the rain, mud, scorching days, cold nights, and constant harassment from the townspeople.

There was lots of craziness, too. Things I shouldn't write in a letter to a fifteen year old. I'll just say I'd rather keep my clothes on in public thank you. Margie, the energy I felt being with all those women was exhilarating. I think women can change the world. It was amazing how, with so little, those women made that festival a reality. There's already talk of next year.

As far as books, here's a few of my favorites, Maya Angelou - "I Know Why the Caged Bird Sings," Harper Lee - "To Kill A Mockingbird," Truman Capote - "In Cold Blood," and F. Scott Fitzgerald – "The Great Gatsby." They're not all that new, but that should get you started.

Your friend,
Ruth Ann
P.S. I loved "The Outsiders" – Stay Golden!

#

September 3, 1976

Dear Ruth Ann,

Sorry, I haven't written in a while. Ida has been on me like a hawk. I shot my mouth off in Sunday school, but I think I was right. I got into an argument with Old Mr. Gray about his literal interpretation of the bible. Really, there is just some stuff in there that couldn't be true and other stuff that makes no sense now.

He threw me out of class, so the next week Debbie and I got an older guy to buy us some Mad Dog 20/20 wine. If every word in the bible is true then we thought they should be drinking wine at communion and not grape juice. We snuck into the church on Saturday night and switched out the juice. We cut the bottoms off the cans with can openers, replaced the juice with the wine, and then sealed the cans with JB Weld.

It was a genius plan, but when everybody started spitting out the wine during the service, things got a little messy. We got caught because our fingers were tinted purple from the juice. I've been on house arrest for weeks. She even took the door off my room. I finally got that back today after cleaning the garage. She keeps telling me I'm going to hell. Wait till she finds out I'm queer.

The festival sounded cool. I hope I can go someday, if I ever get away from Ida. She did let me go to the library, so I'm reading all the books you suggested. I finished Maya Angelou. She is an incredible writer. I loved it. Thank you! School starts next week. Can't wait for basketball season. I hear there's a new girl moving down here and she's supposed to be good at basketball.

Ida's going to a meeting up the beach, so I can get this mailed today. Have to close now. She's hollering my name again.

Your friend,
Margie

#

September 1976
Chris Evert wins the 96th Women's U.S. Open. Ntozake Shange's "For Colored Girls Who Have Considered Suicide/When the Rainbow Is Enuf" premieres in NYC. American Episcopal Church approves ordination of women as priests & bishop. Playboy releases Jimmy Carter's "lust" interview. "Charlie's Angels" debuts, starring Farrah Fawcett, Kate Jackson, and Jaclyn Smith. "Songs in the Key of Life," the 18th studio album by Stevie Wonder is released.

#

September 26, 1976

Dear Margie,
It's Sunday morning. I'm sitting here at my kitchen table watching the raindrops run down the window. It's hot and muggy with all the windows shut against the rain. I'd rather be there on the beach.

I'm sorry I haven't written in such a long time. Once the semester started, with teaching and taking classes, I haven't had the time to do anything else. I've never been so busy in my life. I still have to do the lecture tours and book signings, as well. It pays the bills, so I have to keep doing it. I would rather stay home and write. I guess you're back in school, by now. How's the sports writing going? You don't have football, do you? What do you write about in the off-season?

The communion wine story was funny. I hope you didn't suffer too much for your irreverence. You are right to question what adults tell you. Educate yourself. Make up your own mind. Speak your truth when you feel strongly enough about something, but you must learn how to frame those words so people will listen. Don't get me wrong, there is a time to shout from the rooftops, but most of the time if you leave someone with a way out, so they can think about what you've said, it works out better. Don't tell them they're wrong; educate them. I'm telling you this, yet, I shoot my mouth off more times than not, so do as I say, not as I do. Ha, ha.

Yes, Maya Angelou is a powerful writer. I'm sure she will be one of the strongest voices in literature for a long time. Keep reading her. She is wise and her poetry is divine. Let me know what you think of the others. You should write a little about each book you read and keep it, in case you have to read it again for school. It helps you remember.

Have a good school year. I look forward to reports of your continuing escapades.

Your friend,
Ruth Ann

#

October 10, 1976

Dear Ruth Ann,

So much has happened since I wrote you last. A new girl, her name is Amy, moved here this year. Her dad is in the Coast Guard, so she moves a lot. She plays basketball. Amy is a little shorter than me, but she can really shoot and she's fast. We've been practicing, without the coach (rules!), and we work great together. I really like her. Debbie is so jealous she can't stand herself. I don't care. She can't have all my attention anymore, besides she has that boyfriend of hers hanging on her all the time. Anyway, I think Amy might be like me, but I'm afraid to ask.

I wrote an article for the paper about Title IX. I got an A on it. I'm sending you a copy. I'm trying to cover sports related stories right now, since we're not playing. I wrote an article about Amy joining the team and some other new boys, last week. Debbie got snotty and said, "It's bad enough you let your little girlfriend follow you around like a puppy dog, now you have to write about her." I think Debbie's screwing her boyfriend.

I finished all those books you suggested. "In Cold Blood," was much better than the movie. The same with "To Kill a Mockingbird." I loved Scout. "Gatsby," too many *stupid women and men being led around by their privates. Suggest some more to read. Outside of basketball, there is nothing to do here in winter but fish. You can only get so cold before that becomes no fun.*

    Your friend,
Margie

#

"The number one soul song this week is 'Just To Be Close To You' by the Commodores. The number one country song, 'You and Me' by Tammy Wynette. And the number one best selling album this week, debuting in the number one position the first week on, Stevie Wonder and Songs in the Key of Life." American Top 40, Broadcast October 16, 1976

#

October 27, 1976

Dear Margie,

    Sounds like your year has already been exciting. Keep me posted on how the basketball season is going. I'm glad you made a new friend. I wouldn't push the lesbian issue. Just let things happen naturally. God, if anybody ever sees these letters I'll be hog-tied and run out on a rail. Anyway, if you bring it up and she doesn't feel the same way, one of two things will occur. You'll pretend it never happened, or she'll never speak to you again. If she does feel the same way she'll let you know. As far as Debbie goes, be careful. It's true what they say, "Hell hath no fury like a woman scorned." That's not the exact quote from Shakespeare, but you get the drift.

    I read the Title IX article. It was very well written and your points were well made. I enjoyed reading it, very much. Keep sending me the stuff you write. As far as more books to read, have you read all the Mark Twain books and short stories? If you haven't, you should. In addition, you should read Ernest Hemingway, Willa Cather, William Faulkner, Carson McCullers, Virginia Woolf, John Steinbeck, and James Joyce, just to name a few. Don't forget to read newspapers and magazines, so you'll know what's happening beyond that little island. That should keep you busy.

Take care.
Your friend,
Ruth Ann

#

November 2, 1976
Democrat candidate Jimmy Carter is elected President of
the United States, defeating incumbent Republican
President Gerald Ford. "If You Leave Me Now" by
Chicago is the number one song on the Billboard chart.

#

November 17, 1976
Dear Ruth Ann,
How are you? I'm doing great. The team is winning. I
scored a career high thirty-two points last night. I just
couldn't miss. Amy took over the point guard position, so I
can be the shooting guard. We're the only starting
sophomores. Everyone else is a senior or junior. I think we
have a chance to win the conference.
You were right about Amy letting me know how she felt.
She is like me. We both have boyfriends to keep the rumors
from starting, but Debbie keeps making stupid remarks. I'm
going to brain her if she keeps it up. Doesn't she know if she
tells about Amy and me that they'll find out about us too? I
don't like the way that sounds. I don't want to feel guilty
about feeling this way. I wish everyone would just mind their
own business.
I started reading Faulkner. My English teacher is
impressed. He wanted to know who was helping me with my
reading list. I told him, "An author friend of mine," and
walked away fast. It made me feel important. I didn't tell him
who you were though. He and Ida are buddies. I hate that I
can't tell people I know you. Nobody would believe I'm
friends with a famous author. I think I might tell Amy. I told
her about your book. She wants to read it, but I'm afraid
she'll get caught with it and I'll get in trouble. Maybe the
next time she spends the night I'll let her read some of it.
Speaking of spending the night, I'm a little confused.
They tell us to keep our virginity until we get married, but

isn't that just so we won't get pregnant? If I can't get pregnant with a girl, then do I still have to wait? It's getting harder to do that. I'm not sure what happens next, but I have a feeling it's going to happen soon. Amy doesn't know either, so it's the blind leading the blind. Are you still a virgin if you've been all the way with a girl, and exactly what is all the way? The worst part is I think I'm in love with Amy, but I don't know if it's the fooling around or her that I really like.

I'm so glad I have you to talk to. I'd go crazy if I didn't. I'm enclosing some articles from the school paper and a few clippings from the sports page of the Coastland Times. There's even a picture of me shooting. That's Amy standing behind me in the picture. I think she's cute.

    Your friend,
    Margie

#

"The number one best selling album again this week, and this is eight weeks in a row, Stevie Wonder and Songs in The Key of Life. And on the Billboard singles chart the number one best selling song again this week in the U. S. A., 'Tonight's the Night,' gonna be all right, Rod Stewart." —American Top 40, Broadcast December 5, 1976

#

December 5, 1976

Dear Margie,

I'm so proud of you. Congratulations on your basketball successes. I check the box scores every Wednesday and Saturday to see how you're doing. Your scores aren't always in there, but I see enough to know you are an amazing basketball player. The recruiters should already be knocking down your door. Do you have any ideas about where you want to play in college? With your grades you can go anywhere, so choose the school that best fits your educational needs. You'll need a career when basketball is over. Your writing in the articles is very good and yes, Amy is cute.

Margie, you're not the first and definitely won't be the last person who can't tell people they know me. Being an out lesbian has actually made it much harder to find friends. Some lesbians and gay men are so far in the closet, they are afraid that being seen with me might expose their secret. The straight people are terrified someone might think they are gay just being in my presence. I wish we could do away with labels, but that's a Utopian way of looking at it. If everybody were out, there would be no need to hide, but until things change a lot of closet doors will remain firmly closed. You're braver than most, and I appreciate your friendship more than you know.

My advice would be to keep your secret. Wait a little while longer. You really are just waking up to your sexuality and things are fluid in those years. Don't declare yourself something now. You'll be stuck with that label. Go out, have fun, experiment, but be careful. You're a smart girl and, I believe, one of good character. Trust yourself. You know right from wrong.

Okay, sleeping with girls... now, this could really get me in hot water, but I'm going to have to trust you, Margie. I know you need help. Lord knows, I wished for someone to talk to when I was your age. I am guessing you're past the rubbing all over each other with your clothes on part. That's the same for boys and girls, by the way. My take on it is just to do what comes naturally. As you grow you'll learn more, but really in the beginning just let things happen. You're discovering your own body at this point, so if it feels good to you, it probably will to her.

Virginity is a misnomer, if you ask me. I knew girls that had done everything imaginable with a boy except the act of penetration, and they still claimed to be virgins. I say bullshit. Don't worry so much about remaining a virgin. There aren't as many out there as claim to be. In the end, when you give your heart and soul to someone, and they give you theirs back, the degree of your virginity won't matter.

Glad you liked Faulkner. He's one of my favorites, but then I'm partial to southern writers. Take care and keep hitting those shots. Merry Christmas and have a Happy New Year!

Your friend,

Ruth Ann
P.S. You should get a package from me sometime soon. Hope you enjoy.

#

December 12, 1976

Dear Ruth Ann,
   I got the package yesterday. Thank you so much. Another autographed copy for my collection. I guess you know the author, since she signed it to me. I like how she signed her pen name and her real name. I started reading Patience and Sarah *last night. It's a great book. Ida saw it and asked what it was about. I told her pioneer women. She believed me. That was close.*
   Don't worry about anyone ever seeing your letters. I don't even keep them in the house. I have a place in the woods where I keep a lockbox in a tree. No one will ever find it.
   I'm sorry it's so hard for you to have friends. At least you have Linda, even though she lives so far away. When I'm older and it won't matter, I'll be proud to stand in public as your friend. Until then, I'll take your advice and stay quiet. That is if I can keep Debbie from squealing. Now, she says if I don't kiss her she'll tell. That really doesn't make much sense, but she's not being very rational right now. I have to hide it from Amy, so she won't get mad. I'm being pulled in so many directions; it's hard to concentrate on school.
   We're playing in a holiday tournament over Christmas. We've only lost two games. I couldn't hit the broadside of a barn and neither could anyone else. I'm a shepherd in the Christmas play at church because they ran out of boys. Amy is the Virgin Mary. Debbie was always Mary, but this year she's the narrator. It's crazy being in church with the two of them making eyes at me and hating each other. Ida asked me why Debbie didn't hang out at the house anymore. I told her it was because she was so wrapped up in boys.
   I hope you like the gift. Merry Christmas and Happy New Year. See you in '77.
   Your friend,
   Margie

#

"Wonder Woman" debuts on ABC, December 18, 1976.
On December 28th, Winnie Mandela is banished in South
Africa.

#

December 27, 1976

Dear Margie,

Hope you had a great Christmas. Just dropping a note to
say thank you for the silver surfboard keychain. It has my
keys on it already. Glad you liked Patience and Sarah. *It's a*
sweet story. Back to the classics with you. Hope your
holidays go well.

Have a great New Year,
Ruth Ann

Chapter Two

"1977"

January 2, 1977

Dear Ruth Ann,
You are never going to believe what happened. We got out of school on Dec. 17th. (I made all A's, by the way.) We had a game that night and then I went home with Amy. Her parents were gone for the weekend. I convinced Ida that we were making homemade tree ornaments and wouldn't she rather me mess up someone else's kitchen, so she let me go. I'm not going into detail here, but I got my Christmas present from Amy that weekend. Wow!

We did make the plaster ornaments, but mostly we just, well, you know. Anyway, we had to go to church on Sunday and I was sure I would burst into flames when I went in the door, but nothing happened. Then we had Christmas Pageant practice that afternoon. Amy, Debbie, and me were the oldest girls in the pageant. We have to move to the junior choir next year. We were changing into our costumes in this little room. Two freshmen girls were in there, too.

Suddenly, Debbie screams, "What's that?" and points at my neck. I have no idea what she's talking about. I thought a spider or something was on me, so I started jumping around, swatting my neck. Then she says, "It's not a bug. You have a hickey on your neck."

I tried to remain as calm as possible, but I really wanted to run. I looked over at Amy and she was studying her costume, as if it was some kind of puzzle, and pretending she hadn't heard a word of what Debbie said.

I said, "It can't be a hickey. I must have rubbed on a branch in the woods."

"That's a hickey, Margie, and I bet I know who gave it to you." Debbie screamed that so loud I thought someone would come bursting through the door any minute. Then totally out of the blue she charged at Amy and pushed her down. By now, Debbie was crying and any attempt I made to get her quiet just made her louder.

She yelled at Amy, "Why did you have to come here? Everything was fine before you came."

Now, you have to know Amy knew nothing about Debbie, other than she'd been a bitch to her. She thought it was because I was Debbie's friend before, and nothing else. Well, she knows everything now, because Debbie turned on me after she got done with Amy, and said, "I'm going to tell your mother."

I forgot about the other two girls in the room. I also forgot that Amy didn't know about Debbie and me. I shot my mouth off, "Yeah, well if you tell about me and Amy, then I'm telling about you and me."

The next thing I knew, they were both trying to kill me. Amy broke the shepherd's staff over my head and Debbie tried to beat me to death with the Baby Jesus. They didn't stop whacking me until they realized the two freshmen girls were trying to escape. They let me go and tackled the other two. After some serious threatening we let the other girls go. I think we scared them really bad. Debbie told them we'd sneak in their rooms at night and cut off their hair if they told. If they've spoken a word of what was said in that room, I haven't heard it. If those girls ever wise up and realize they can blackmail us, we're in deep shit.

After pageant practice, Amy wouldn't speak to me and neither would Debbie. I was so mad at Debbie. She ruined everything. I tried to talk to Amy on Monday, but her mom said she was sick and couldn't come to the door. I went home and stole Ida's green food coloring. I snuck into Debbie's house and put the dye in her favorite green apple shampoo. Her brothers would have had to take the blame, if Ida hadn't decided to make Christmas tree cookies and couldn't find the green food coloring. She put two and two together after talking to Debbie's mom at the store.

So, to make a long story short, Amy quit talking to me, Debbie was a bitch with green hair, and I had blue hair, because that's what Ida had in her hand when she attacked me in the shower after she got back from her little chat with Debbie's mom. Thank god, she didn't see the hickey. It's gone now. We all appeared in the pageant together, after a talking to by the preacher about forgiveness. I think Debbie's green hair contrasted very nicely with her all white angel costume, but her wings were still bent from the fight the week before. Both Baby Jesus and my shepherd's staff benefitted from the healing powers of Duct tape. Ida didn't manage to get all my hair, but the bright blue stripe down the middle of my scalp was less than appealing. The dye has faded some now, but you can still see it.

Amy finally started speaking to me again a few days after Christmas. I told her I was sorry that I didn't tell her about Debbie and I think she understood. We talked about what people would say if they found out. We decided to head off the rumors by sleeping with our boyfriends. We didn't go all the way, but just enough to give them something to talk about. I endured a night of groping and pawing. Boys are not very good at that sort of thing in my opinion, but it worked. We're now sluts. I can't win for losing, but at least they don't tar and feather the sluts. We're more popular than ever.

School starts back tomorrow. I read Hemingway and Steinbeck over the holiday. They wrote so much; I think I'll switch to someone else for a while. I also read, "The Children's Hour," by Lillian Hellman. Were you saving that for later? I wanted to strangle that little girl. I loved it, but why are the lesbians always so sad? Oh, by the way, we won the holiday tournament and I played in it with blue hair. I didn't mind. Debbie had to cheer with her green hair. Her skin was kind of green too and since our school colors are green and gold, she looked like Gumby with pompons.

Your friend,
Margie

#

January 4, 1977, Mary Shane hired by Chicago White Sox as 1st woman TV play-by-play. Jacqueline Means is the 1st woman formally ordained an Episcopal priest. "You Don't Have to be A Star" by Marilyn McCoo and Billy Davis, Jr. is at the top of the Billboard chart.

#

January 9, 1977

Dear Margie,

I just read your last letter. I haven't laughed that hard in a long time. Thank God for Duct tape. You had a very busy holiday it appears. Remind me never to make you angry. I'd hate to wind up shorn of hair or with rainbow locks. I am glad things worked out okay.

I spent Christmas at my folks' house and endured my own form of torture. My mother still insists there's time to change me, before I'm old and regret not marrying and having children. I don't think I'll ever teach that old dog a new trick. Her friends at the country club, if they don't shudder in disgust at my presence, are often flirting slyly. If I see another gray haired woman wink at me, I may scream. I also saw the girl with whom I had my first lesbian experiences in high school. She's married with two kids at her heals and a baby on her hip. Hence, my warning to be careful about falling too hard when you're young. People change. In her case it was a lot. She would barely make eye contact with me. Sometimes I wish I had never written that book.

I went to the Governor's Inauguration Ball for James Hunt. My parents insisted that I attend in full ball gown and heels with an appropriate escort. Really, my mother threw a fit and fell in it and if I wanted peace, I had to go. The date was an old friend that met Mother's criteria. He is sweet, charming, drop dead gorgeous and rich. Mother doesn't know he's gay, too. It was a lovely evening, but alas, I would have rather been in jeans and a tee shirt on the beach.

I'm packing now to leave this week for the Presidential Inauguration. I'm covering the feminist and lesbian delegations and groups. I'm trying to get a line on how they feel the new administration will deal with the ERA issue and gay people in general. I am hopeful that Carter will continue to move forward on both. The University is covering my classes so I can do this trip. The dean thinks it's good for the department to be involved first hand in the Women's Movement, since that's what we're discussing in class. I got lucky with this job. I was afraid after I came out, I'd never get a teaching position. It's a shame, but you really need to think about those things, as you get older. Don't let them label you, Margie, but sleeping with guys has its own problems. You do know how to be safe and careful, I hope.

My holiday was not a complete loss. I did go to Chicago to visit Linda. She says hello. We spent New Year's together in her apartment. (My birthday is Jan. 1st.) Even Linda, the radical feminist, can't be seen with me in public. She's an on air personality and is easily recognized in Chicago. I really didn't mind. After a week with my mother, I was glad for the peace and quiet. I might be a lesbian, but according to Mother, I'm a famous one so she doesn't mind parading me all over town. Actually, when the book came out along with me, after the initial shock and threats of deadly violence, she took to being the expert mother of the famous lesbian author. Fame is fame in her mind, I guess.

The way you told that story, you really could be a writer. In fact, you already are. Keep writing down your tales. I wish I had written more at your age. It would have helped when I was writing the book. Your life is your story. Record it for the years down the road when you want to remember how you arrived at where you are. I arrived here, in Chapel Hill, on this rainy, icy, afternoon, by a culmination of events that filled my life with both joy and sorrow, but mostly laughter. What happens to you, what is said to and about you, the people you meet, the decisions you make all shape you into what you will become. Take note of these events. It will make it easier to understand yourself, when you're older. Until next time...

Your friend,
Ruth Ann

#

January 23, 1977, the mini-series "Roots" premieres on ABC. Rose Royce has the number one Billboard single, "Car Wash"

#

January 30, 1977

Dear Ruth Ann,

It's been a while since I've written, because I've just been swamped. Between basketball, school, Debbie, Amy, and dodging Ida's questions, I've been really busy. Debbie's mom thinks she's having sex with her boyfriend, (she is,) so Ida thinks I am too. I'd tell her the truth just to get her off my back, but I don't think telling her about Amy would go over very well, either. I told Ida, I'm fighting him off, and I am, every time we're alone. I should have never let him think I would do it with him. He can't understand why I'm not letting him do anything, since that one time. I told him I was afraid I would get pregnant. That slowed him down some. Amy and me double date with the guys, which is not much. We go to the movies a few times a month and school dances, but that's about it. We try not to be alone with them any more than we have to. Debbie's boyfriend is a Junior. He drives, so they go out and screw all the time. I'm glad she likes guys. She can have my share. I just don't understand why she's still mad at me over Amy. She's got him. What does she need me for?

Happy Birthday! I didn't know or I would have sent you something. I'm glad you got to spend it with Linda. I would have liked to see you in your ball gown. I bet you were beautiful. I need a gay guy like that for a boyfriend. Then I wouldn't have to spend the entire movie trying to keep his hand off my boob. I had to see "Rocky" twice to know what was happening. I thought it was because I was distracted with the hand/boob war the first time, but the second time I realized Stallone mostly said only the vowels. I saw "All The President's Men," too, and now I know I want to be a reporter.

Our English teacher is making us keep a journal this semester. I write about surfing and stuff. I can't really write about what I'm thinking. It would definitely shock old Mrs. Whitley. She said she wouldn't read them, if we didn't want her to, but I don't believe her. Would you?

Basketball is going well. We're second in the conference. Maybe if we make the State tournament in Raleigh you could come and watch me play. I hope we make it. I did get a letter from Chapel Hill about basketball. Wouldn't it be great if I ended up there? I could take your class. We'll see. My dad really wants me to go to State and play for Kay Yow. I like Old Dominion, too. Have you seen Nancy Lieberman play? She was the youngest player on the Olympic team. They call her Lady Magic. She's really good. If I go to ODU, she would be a senior my freshman year. That would be cool.

When basketball season is over, Amy is going to teach me how to play tennis. She played in Florida at her last school. I like tennis. I watch it on TV. How hard can it be? Evert is my favorite player. I don't like that Martina girl. She whines too much. Besides, Chrissy is so much cuter.

Well, I guess I've talked your ear off. I'm still reading the authors you suggested. Once I've read everything I'll let you know what I thought. I started making note cards for each book, so we can talk about them when you're here this summer. I can't wait. See you soon.

Your friend,
Margie

#

On February 2, 1977, Iris Rivera is fired for refusing to make coffee for her boss. Her dismissal leads to Women Employed bringing 50 women to her office to stage a coffee-making lesson for the lawyers. The instructions included "Step 5: Turn on the switch." The demonstration made the front page of the paper and led to her reinstatement. And on top of the Billboard charts is Mary MacGregor with "Torn Between Two Lovers."

#

February 16, 1977

Dear Margie,

I have been running like a chicken with its head cut off since I got back from D.C. I finally forced myself to stop and write to you. I read in the paper that your team is in the playoffs. If you make it to State, I will most definitely be there. I have to pull for UNC on the recruitment issue. We do have a fine journalism school here, but you need to go where you will feel the most comfortable. I did see Lieberman play last year at an ODU game, as a matter of fact. You are quite correct. She is an amazing player to watch.

I do play tennis; after all, what good southern girl brought up in the country club can't swing a racket, or a club, or both. I also like Chris Evert, but I think Martina is just going to get better. She's very young and strong as an ox. I'd like to see her play in person. What you call whiny other people call competiveness. People from places like Czechoslovakia and Russia are passionate in their speech. Read some Chekov. I don't think we should judge her emotional court play by American standards. Even so, McEnroe is the worst whiner ever.

The inauguration was a blast. It was one party after another. I didn't mind the high heels so much. After years of backlash from the Nixon administration against the feminist movement of the late sixties and early seventies, a second wave of feminism is said to be lurking with the support of the new administration. Everyone seems to believe the ERA will become a reality under Carter. I have my doubts, but the air of optimism was enticing. Aretha Franklin sang at the inauguration. I guess you probably watched it on TV. Let me just say, it was an extremely patriotic experience for me. The President said, in his speech, "I have no new dream to set forth today, but rather urge a fresh faith in the old dream." I have renewed my faith in America. I believe that one day we will all have equal rights, not only in the form of a written law, but in practice as well.

About the guys, you can always do what I did. When one of them got to be too hard to keep off me, I would find some excuse to break up with him, wait a while, and then find a new one. It takes each one a little time to build up the courage to try anything, so it'll give you a break. I can't explain why Debbie is still mad, other than she obviously isn't happy with the way things turned out for her. I've known women like her, too. They don't really want you and they're not really gay, but they sure do chase you around, don't they? You might as well learn how to deal with the "straight girl" trolling now. My advice, stay clear. They are nothing but trouble. However, as I say this, I am reminded that Linda was a straight girl, too. So, who knows? Women are nuts is the best I can figure.

With those words of wisdom, I bid you adieu. That reminds me; what foreign language are you taking? You should take Latin next year. If they don't offer it at your high school, let me know. I can get you in a correspondence course and I'll teach you. You won't regret it. Your test scores will go through the roof and writing will become so much easier. I know you really don't want to read the classics, but you should also be studying the Greeks. You'll get some exposure in class, but not enough. You'll learn everything you ever needed to know about structure from those old stories.

Okay, enough of the lecture on academics. I am counting the weeks to the summer. I plan to surf every day, with you, if you can tear yourself away from Amy. Ha, ha. See you soon.

Your friend,
Ruth Ann

#

The three songs atop the Billboard chart February 26, 1977 are:
1. "New Kid in Town" – Eagles
2. The theme from "A Star Is Born" – Barbra Streisand
3. "Blinded By The Light" – Manfred Mann's Earth Band

#

March 1, 1977

Dear Ruth Ann,

I am so bored. This is the first Tuesday since December that I haven't had a game to play in. We lost in the last game that would have sent us to the State Championship in Raleigh. I guess there's always next year, but we better get a big girl to move down here or somebody is going to have to grow. I'm five-nine(I grew an inch since last summer) and the tallest one left. I am not going to play under the basket. Dad said he would try to find a job on the mainland, so I could get more looks from the recruiters, but I said no. If they want me then they'll just have to come down here and get me. Besides, I couldn't leave Amy behind.

Dad asked me to think about applying to West Point, because they started taking women last year. I don't think I'd be a good fit for the military. I've lived with Ida long enough to know I hate taking orders. And don't they kick gay people out of the military? I read that article about the sergeant in Time magazine, last year. I don't want to leave here and have to hide for another six years. I told him I didn't want to go because their basketball team wasn't any good. I think he bought it.

I took your advice and dumped the boyfriend. The problem is we don't have too many guys down here to choose from, so I have to space them out to make them last until I graduate or hope for more Coast Guard transfers. I only have to make it a couple of more months and then we'll be out of school and I can be done with boys for the summer. The guys around here like to hit on tourist girls, so they'll leave us alone. Debbie has been better. She had a pregnancy scare and backed off the boyfriend quite a bit. She hangs out with Amy and me sometimes, now. She just seems real sad.

I've been saving money from odd jobs so I can buy a wet suit. Then I don't have to wait for the water to warm up. I'll probably have enough in a month, because I have more free time now that basketball is over. I play softball too, but it doesn't take up as much time as basketball. Our softball team is okay, but we haven't had a team for very long and it's going to take some time for the girls down here to start playing like they do everywhere else. I read a lot about the softball programs in "WomenSports Magazine."

I guess you're right about Martina Navratilova. She's really strong and I like the way she charges the net. I love Evert, but all those long strokes can get boring. It's always exciting to watch Martina play. Amy starts my tennis lessons next week. Who knows, maybe I'll be good at that, too. I hope I learn enough to play a set with you when you come down. By the way, I read "The Cherry Orchard." You're right; those folks are very dramatic. Ida would fit right in with all the lamenting.

I read, "A Streetcar Named Desire," too. They sure left a lot of that story out of the movie and the same with "Cat on a Hot Tin Roof." Why in the world would anybody understand why Skipper killed himself if they didn't read the play? They talk so much between the lines in the movie. In the play, it's all just right there. I got the uncensored version from the librarian. She's cool. She ordered "Orlando" for me, but made me promise not to tell Ida. I can't wait to read it. I'll just tell Ida it's a book about Florida; she won't know the difference. Ida's not dumb, but she won't read Walt Whitman because she says it's trash. So, I doubt seriously she knows who Virginia Woolf is. Ida's more of an Agatha Christie reader.

I can't believe I wrote so much. You must be tired of reading by now. I'll let you go. Thanks for writing. It helps to have a friend I can just talk to, and I certainly couldn't talk to anyone else about the whole lesbian thing. I hope we'll be friends forever.

Your friend always,
Margie
P.S. The librarian is going to teach me Latin next year. The school is paying for the correspondence course. Thanks for the idea.

#

March 17, 1977

Dear Margie,

Sorry about the basketball team not making State. I saw where you made All-State in your division. That is quite a feat for a sophomore. Congratulations. The schools are going to be knocking down your door. You are smart, fast, and shoot like Pistol Pete. I'm sure you'll have your choice of scholarships. That's also great news about the Latin class. You will not regret it, I promise.

I absolutely adore Tennessee Williams. I'm glad you read those two plays. They are my favorites. The detailed scenery description for "Cat" is so beautifully written, it's a work of art in itself. You should read his biography. He and Truman Capote were quite the party pair in New York. If you like Virginia Woolf, you should read "Mrs. Dalloway" and "To the Lighthouse."

Now, on to tennis. You better practice. I'm going to mop the court with you. Maybe I can teach you a thing or two about tennis in exchange for more surfing lessons. I wasn't completely forthcoming earlier. I played tennis in college. I'm not too bad. I should be able to give you some pointers. So, you practice hard and when I get there we'll see how far you've come. One tip: Don't rely on the two handed backhand. The one handed is more reliable if you're strong enough, and it gives you more range. I think you're plenty strong.

Well, I have to get to bed now. You take care and I'll write as often as I can, but I'm going to be really busy for the rest of the spring, so don't worry if it takes some time between letters. I will write back, I promise.

Your friend always, too,
Ruth Ann

#

The 1976–1977 season marked the release of the first AP Poll for women's basketball. On March 26, 1977, Delta State won its third straight AIAW Women's Basketball Tournament Championship, beating LSU in the final. Pat Head, who had her first twenty win season in her third year as head coach, lead Tennessee over Immaculata in the consolation game. On April 2, 1977, Fleetwood Mac's "Rumours" album hits number one.

#

April 3, 1977

Dear Ruth Ann,

I can play tennis. I like it a lot. I think I like it better than softball. I need help with the overhead serve. I keep hitting it out of the tennis court fence. Amy has tried to teach me, but I just can't get over the top of the ball. Every now and then I hit it just right and wow! This game is fun. I'll keep working at it.

I understand about you being busy. You don't have to write back every time I write you, just whenever you can.

I did some work for my dad and he bought the wet suit for me. I haven't tried it out in the water, yet. I just got it yesterday. I did wear it for several hours just to get the feel of it. Amy thought I was an idiot for walking around the house in a wet suit, but it was fun. We laughed a lot. I laugh all the time with Amy. I think that's why I like her so much. We're going to try to go to the same college. I have to make up my mind, so she can start planning how she will get there. She makes straight A's, too. Her test scores are good enough for any of the schools I'm looking at. She can't go the private school route without a full scholarship. That knocks out ODU. UNC is looking better all the time.

Amy's parents want her to go to a junior college. She has two little sisters, both in elementary school. Her dad is in the Coast Guard and her mom stays at home. Her dad keeps encouraging her to join the Navy and then go to school on the G. I. Bill. I wonder why both our dads are pushing us toward the military? I'm not doing it and neither is Amy. I told her we'd figure something out. We have two more years.

I finally told Amy about you. She was so excited. I don't let her read your letters, though. That's just between you and me. Amy read The Belle Cracked at my house, over a couple of weekends. She would laugh all night. I had to keep telling her to be quiet, so she didn't wake Ida. Now, she wants to read "Rubyfruit Jungle." She said she had no idea there were books like that out there. She said she read a lesbian smut book once, but that this was the first time the characters seemed like real people, girls like us. I didn't know there were lesbian smut books, so she's one up on me. Maybe that's why she knew what to do.

Well, I have to go. Dad's taking me down to the beach this afternoon to try out the wet suit. He can take me where the break is, in his truck. Plus, Ida won't let me go without him. She says I'll freeze and drown. I might wish I had gotten booties and gloves, but I don't think I'll freeze. Anyway, have a good Easter.

Friends always,
Margie
P.S. What is all this Anita Bryant mess about?

#

May 2, 1977

Dear Margie,

I can't believe I let almost a month go by without writing you. I'm preparing for my exams. I feel pretty good about all my classes. Taking a full load of graduate courses and teaching did not make this an easy year, but I survived. I just have to give the final in the class I teach, score it, turn in the grades and then I'm done. I'll be finished with exams by next week and then I'm off to Florida.

In your last letter, you asked about Anita Bryant. Funny you should mention her. I am going down to cover the campaign against the ordinance in Dade County that would prevent people from being denied basic human rights based on sexual preference. The opposition to the bill is being led by the Save Our Children group. Anita was the spokesperson, but she drew so much bad publicity she has stepped into the background a little more. Her basic stance is what you do in your home is your business, but don't be proud to be a homosexual, don't let other people know your sexuality, and certainly don't tell the children that it's okay to feel that way. The story has drawn national attention. This should be an interesting month.

I'm driving down and taking my surfboard. How was the wet suit? Did you freeze your boobs off? I can't wait to hit the ocean. I'll be in Miami, so I'm having my mail forwarded, but you know how slow that can be. I'm coming back here after the vote, the first week in June. Then it will be less than a month until I arrive in Buxton for a much needed rest. Linda is coming, too. I haven't seen her since February, but we talk on the phone a lot.

You don't want to hear this next part, but I need to say it. I know that you might think that you and Amy are going to go merrily along through life, just as you are now. That may well be the case, but in most instances it is not. Don't base where you go to college on whether Amy can come with you or not. By the time you get to that college, Amy will probably be long gone, and then you'll be stuck at a school you chose for the wrong reasons. I am not making light of your feelings for each other. I know they are real. Let's just say, I'm speaking from a more enlightened position. Relationships come and go. You have to be true to your dreams. A lot is going to change over the next few years. Other people change, too, remember that.

Please don't think I'm pulling the "I'm an adult and you're a child" routine on you. I'm not. I've just been there.

See you soon.

Friends always,

Ruth Ann

#

"Moving into the top position this week is Leo Sayer, 'When I Need You.' And there you have it, the most popular song in the nation."— American Top 40, Broadcast May 14, 1977.

#

May 15, 1977

Dear Ruth Ann,

Hope you're having fun in Florida. I wish I was there. I'd rather be anywhere but here, right now. I'm on restriction until Ida gets tired of badgering me, which could be never. I can't see Amy or Debbie, for at least a month, outside of Church and school. The worst part is it wasn't our fault.

The senior girls decided to throw a party on the beach for all the underclassman. I was suspicious, but Amy said we had to go. We dragged Debbie with us. We thought she could use the party, besides she is sixteen now and can drive. I don't drink alcohol or smoke pot and neither does Amy, but Debbie does. She thinks it's cool. I think I'd rather Ida not kill me. Of course, the seniors were going to try and get us drunk and make us do stupid shit. I knew it, but I couldn't let Amy go by herself, and I thought Debbie could use a drink. She's really depressed.

Ten of us showed up. One girl picked us up at the campground, in a truck, and took us out on the beach. There were eight seniors standing by this fire with a cooler and paper cups. In the cooler they had mixed Everclear with fruit punch. Cut up oranges and lemons floated around on top. They called it Purple Jesus, because "if you drank enough you could talk to God." They gave us each a cup and we started drinking. That stuff goes down pretty fast after a few cups. At first, they just told us things about teachers and classes we would take before we graduated. I didn't mind the insight, really, but then they started talking about boys, which quickly went downhill to talking about sex.

I played along like I knew what they were talking about, but I just don't get the big deal about boys. Debbie and Amy played along too, but I think they really do know more about sex with boys than I do. Well, I know Debbie does. I haven't asked Amy about it. I didn't think she'd done that with a guy. I kind of don't want to know. Does that make sense to you?

Anyway, the evening progressively got worse from there. The seniors made us all go down to the water. They said we were going skinny dipping. I thought that was a very bad idea, but I was too drunk to stop myself. I guess that's what alcohol does to your brain. The seniors were getting undressed too, so I figured they weren't setting us up or anything. Boy was I wrong. They got in the water first and then we all followed them. I realized, too late, that the seniors all got out when we got in. By the time I got back to the beach, all of our clothes were gone and so were the seniors.

We were on the south side of the point, near the campground. We started walking. It was about a half a mile hike. By the time we got near the dunes, I had sobered up quite a bit but I couldn't say the same for the rest of them. The ones that weren't throwing up were crying by then, except for Amy, who just kept giggling, and Debbie, who was as mad as I was, but still drunk.

It was getting late and we had to get to Amy's house. That's where we were all supposed to be staying. The three of us left the others in the dunes and snuck down to the campground. Debbie's car was there, but her keys were in her jeans. There were a few people camping so we decided to steal whatever we could find to cover ourselves. We planned to bring it all back in the morning. We never got the chance.

We saw a tee shirt and two towels drying on a tent line. We were almost there when screams erupted from the dunes behind us. I turned around and here came the other seven girls, running and screaming like something was after them. There was something after them. The senior girls were coming over the ramp from the beach in the pickup truck, which now contained some of their boyfriends, as well. All the screaming woke up the campers and alerted the park rangers. When the headlights from the pickup and the ranger trucks hit those girls, they scattered like roaches through the campground. Some of them even ran into the swamp on the back side. I wish I had gone with them. They got away.

Unfortunately, I couldn't move. When all the screaming started, Amy and Debbie both latched onto me and froze. We were pinned in the headlights of the ranger truck shortly after that. There I was stark naked with two equally naked girls wrapped around me. The good news is they did not arrest us. The bad news is they brought me home to Ida. I think my dad was laughing, but Ida was so wound up I really couldn't look at him long. I had to keep dodging things Ida was throwing at me.

So, here I sit in my room, plotting my revenge. I don't know when I'll get a chance to mail this letter. I hope I'll be off restriction by the time you get here.

Your friend the prisoner,

Margie

#

May 22, 1977

Dear Ruth Ann,

I just had to write and tell you that we got our revenge and, although I am on some kind of double house arrest, it was worth it. Last night was the Junior-Senior Prom. Amy and I didn't go, but Debbie did. Her boyfriend is a junior. He was pretty pissed about the seniors taking our clothes too, so he helped. His name is Jerry. I think a lot more of him now than I did before. He's really kind of sweet.

My mom and dad were chaperones at the prom, so I could sneak out of the house. Amy's parents go to bed as soon as the little ones go down so she met me behind the school. Jerry and Debbie let us in the back door by the cafeteria and helped us find a ladder. We went into the cafeteria and climbed through the ceiling until we were over the girls bathroom.

Debbie told the seniors that we weren't mad about them stealing our clothes and that Jerry had given her a bottle of Vodka. She told them he hid it above the ceiling tiles in the girls bathroom and that she needed their help getting it down. They're all lushes so they were glad to help. This was right before they were scheduled to crown the king and queen. I knew the one who had talked the most that night on the beach would be the queen and some of the others would be her court.

In the meantime, Jerry was helping us fill water balloons in the cafeteria kitchen and transport them over the ceiling tiles to the bathroom. Then he went back into the prom. When Debbie got all the girls in the bathroom, she pointed at the ceiling tile above the toilet farthest from the door. The seniors all went to the stall, while Debbie snuck out the door. She and Jerry held the door shut from outside.

Amy and I popped the ceiling tiles out and pelted those girls till all their Farrah hair was dripping wet and their makeup was running down their faces. Not to mention that their dresses were hanging off them like wet paper bags. We ran, but it was no use. They knew who had done it. We didn't try to hide who we were. We thought about it, but knew everyone would know it was us anyway. I was home watching TV when they caught up with me.

I don't even care that Ida is fit to be tied. Those twits got what they deserved. My Dad and Ida have been arguing all day about it. Dad is on my side, but Ida will win I'm sure.

I'm putting this letter in with the one from last week. I have not had a chance to mail it yet, but Amy said she could mail it for me and check my box after school tomorrow. Her parents weren't quite as mad as Ida about any of this. Glad I went to the library. I have plenty to read. From the sounds downstairs, I may not get out of this room for a long time.

Still your friend the prisoner,
Margie

#

June 10, 1977, Lusia Harris, 6'3" center from Delta State University, is awarded the first Broderick Cup as the most outstanding athlete in the AIAW. She becomes the first woman "officially" drafted in the NBA when the New Orleans Jazz calls her name in the seventh round. Harris declined to try out.

#

June 12, 1977

Dear Margie,

I just arrived back from Florida. First, the surfing was great. It took me a little while to get my feet back under me, but I finally did. I surfed almost every day. You would have been in heaven.

Sorry about all your troubles. I think the seniors got what they deserved, as well. Good job, by the way. No permanent damage was done and that's always a good thing. I'm sure Ida will cool off eventually. My mother always did. You'll probably be free by the time you get this letter. If you're not out by the time I get there, I guess I'll have to organize a jailbreak.

I'll get there on Friday, July first. I'm in the same unit, out by the beach. I'll tell you all about Anita Bryant. I interviewed her. All in all, it was a fun trip, except the bill did not pass. Too much homophobia and misinformation and in reality, some economic issues the author's of the bill did not anticipate.

I'm bringing my tennis racket, so I hope you're ready to play. See you very soon.

Love,

Ruth Ann

#

June 25, 1977

Casey Kasem on American Top 40, Broadcast June 25, 1977. "American Top 40 is heard coast to coast and around the world each week on great radio stations like WYNG-Goldsboro, North Carolina, WHPC-Canton, Ohio, WKBO-Harrisburg, Pennsylvania. The song at number four for the second week in a row is by Foreigner, half-English, half-American. Their song, 'Feels Like The First Time.'"

On this day, Margie Whooten turned sixteen.

Chapter Three

Six days later…

She signed the letter, "Love, Ruth Ann." Margie stared at the signature. "Love, Ruth Ann," said so much in three words. Margie was important to Ruth Ann. She was her friend, not just an amusing teenager. It meant Margie had a place in Ruth Ann's life. It made her feel special and Margie liked that feeling.

She was perched on top of the wooden steps leading up and over the dune to the beach, but facing the motel parking lot. Nearby, pairs of tennis shoes, flip flops, and even a pair of leather men's lace up dress shoes waited for their owners to return. People left their shoes here and no one would bother them. The island was like that. There wasn't a lot of theft. Margie left her bike by the motel office, absolutely sure it would be there when she returned. Islanders knew how small the community was and how fast information could fly. It prevented a lot of light of day shananigans. There aren't a lot of places to hide when everyone can see you.

Now a licensed driver, as of a week ago, Margie still rode her bike everywhere. Ida wasn't about to let a juvenile delinquent drive a motor vehicle. Particularly one who had shown the world her naked body and then attacked helpless girls in a restroom. Ida was still a little hot about all that, but had given in when Bob said enough was enough, and set her free at the end of the second week of June. It had been a hard four weeks. The only highlight had been Ruth Ann's letter that she now carefully refolded and stuck in her pocket.

Margie had been on the lookout since one o'clock. Ruth Ann did not indicate what time she would arrive. Margie fought the urge to come down to the motel all morning, until she could no longer stand it. She knew she would appear too eager. It would certainly lay bare her immaturity. Unable to wait for Ruth Ann to check in and get settled, here she was barging in. Margie couldn't help herself. She'd waited for this moment for fifty weeks. The anticipation was so much worse, now that the moment was close at hand. It was three o'clock. Surely Ruth Ann would be here soon.

Amy's voice behind her turned Margie's head. She had blown Amy off to wait for Ruth Ann. Margie saw Amy every day. She only saw Ruth Ann for two weeks out of the year. Margie thought Amy could hang out at the lighthouse with Debbie or something, just for today, but here she was, standing right in front of Margie with a very unhappy look on her face. *God, girls are so moody*, Margie thought. If Debbie and Amy were any indication, they were extremely jealous, too.

"Didn't your girlfriend get here yet?" Amy repeated, her dark hair blowing into her mouth as she spoke.

She peeled the strands out of the corner of her lips and flipped her long hair away from her face, revealing big brown eyes that so fascinated Margie. As captivating as Amy might be, Margie had grown irritated with all the snide remarks of late. It was as if Amy just wanted to pick a fight, any fight, and the less attention Margie paid to her fits of whatever it was, the angrier Amy had become. Still, when she smiled at Margie, in her better moods, Amy was irresistible. This was such a special day. Margie didn't want to spend it fighting with Amy. She patted the step beside her.

"Here, come sit with me." She waited for Amy to sit down. She bumped her knee up against Amy's and said, "Hey, what's eating you?"

"You left me at the lighthouse with downer Debbie to come up here and meet some woman you're infatuated with. That's what's the matter."

"Amy, you know how much Ruth Ann means to me. We've talked about this. She's my friend and I haven't seen her since last summer. I just thought I should meet her today, that's all."

"It's like you're hiding me," Amy said, her bottom lip began to tremble.

Margie absolutely could not take it when Amy cried, especially if it was because of something she had done. She slipped an arm around Amy's shoulder and pulled her closer. No one would think twice about an attractive girl comforting another. Margie was growing wise to what behaviors they could get away with in public. They were "too pretty" to be gay in most of these people's minds. Yeah, a lot they knew.

"Ruth Ann knows all about you," Margie said. "I talk about you in my letters. She can't wait to meet you. I just wanted to see her first, that's all."

"I'm sorry," Amy said, as she stared at the ground. "I'll go. We can talk tomorrow."

"What's wrong with right now? I'm just sitting here." Margie really wanted to find out what had been going on with Amy, lately.

Amy took a deep breath and looked into Margie's eyes. Whatever it was, it was bad. Margie could see the pain in those brown eyes she loved so much.

"Amy, what's going on?"

Just then a short burst on a car horn sounded very near, startling both of them. Margie, so concentrated on Amy, had not noticed the car pulling up to the last cottage on the end. Ruth Ann climbed out of the front seat with a broad smile on her face. Margie remembered how absolutely stunning she was in person. She had only the grainy black and white photo on the cover of her novel to help remember what Ruth Ann looked like. Over the months Margie's memories of Ruth Ann's face had started to fade. It all came flooding back like a giant wave and slammed into her chest.

Margie loved Amy, of that she had no doubt, but Ruth Ann was something on a whole other plane. Ruth Ann was Margie's ideal, her fantasy. She wavered back and forth between wanting to be Ruth Ann and wanting to love her. It was a primal attraction Margie could not control any more than she could control the color her eyes. She gave into it immediately. Even though she knew she shouldn't leave Amy sitting there alone, her body rose and headed for Ruth Ann.

Ruth Ann was wearing jeans, a white tee shirt tucked in at the waist, and barefooted. It was a rugged and sexy look that Margie hadn't seen before and it worked well against Ruth Ann's tanned skin and dark hair. This time there was no awkward hand shake. Ruth Ann spread her arms and Margie flew into them, wrapping her arms around the older woman's waist and resting her head on her shoulder. Ruth Ann hugged her tight and pulled Margie away from her to get a good look.

"Boy, you grew. How tall are you now?" Ruth Ann asked, beaming at Margie with that perfect set of white teeth and full lips.

Margie blushed as her body, thrilled to be touching Ruth Ann, burst into flames from inside. She managed a shy, "Five-nine."

"I love your hair," Ruth Ann said, while brushing Margie's hair off her shoulder.

"Yeah, I got bored while I was on lock down, so I whacked it off one day. Ida took me to the beauty shop and they cleaned it up."

"Shoulder length is the style now. It looks great on you."

"Thanks," Margie gushed.

"You're gorgeous, Margie. You're growing into a beautiful woman. "

Margie blurted out, "I think you're pretty, too," and then, horrified at her exclamation, tried to cover it with, "Where's Linda?"

"She's coming. I left her at the office. She'll be here in a minute." Ruth Ann was still gripping Margie's shoulders, smiling at her. She pulled Margie to her and hugged her again. "It's so good to see you, kid."

The "kid" stung a little, but not much. Margie knew Ruth Ann meant it affectionately, not as a sign of how she thought of Margie. At least that is what she hoped. She sighed into Ruth Ann's hair, "I missed you."

"I see you've found our little friend and she doesn't look so little anymore." Linda walked up from the direction of the motel office. "Wow, Margie. Let me look at you." She smiled taking all of Margie in. "You're not only taller, but you went from being a tomboy to an androgynous young Dietrich in record time. You're beautiful."

Margie blushed again. This time it was bashfulness, not lust. "Thank you," she said, "It's good to see you, too and you're still as pretty as ever."

Linda cocked her head and raised an eyebrow, "What has my friend here been teaching you about how to charm a woman?"

Ruth Ann laughed. "Oh, I didn't teach her that. She's a natural."

Margie suddenly remembered Amy and panicked. She turned around thinking surely Amy was long gone by now, but she was still sitting on the steps. Amy's mouth had dropped open and she appeared to be frozen in place.

Margie turned back to Ruth Ann. "Hang on a minute. There's someone I want you to meet."

She took long, fast strides over to Amy. Margie stopped in front of her, with her back still turned to Ruth Ann and Linda, so they couldn't see or hear what she was saying. She stuck her hand out to Amy and said, "I know they're gorgeous, but they're just people. Pick your chin up off your chest and come on."

Amy looked up at Margie and silently took her hand. She stood and followed Margie back to the other women.

"Ruth Ann, Linda, this is my girlfriend, Amy." Margie's chest nearly burst with pride when Ruth Ann looked Amy over and then winked at Margie.

"Amy," Ruth Ann began, extending a hand for her to shake, "it is a pleasure to finally meet you. Margie speaks very fondly of you in every letter."

Amy turned to Margie and smiled. Margie smiled back feeling vindicated. Ruth Ann was smooth and she had said just the right thing.

Linda piped in. "My word, Amy, but you're the spitting image of Ruth Ann when she was your age. I've seen the pictures. It's uncanny."

Until that moment, it had not dawned on Margie that Linda was right. Amy did look like Ruth Ann. Why hadn't she seen it before? Maybe it was because she didn't want to think her attraction to Amy had been based on her resemblance to Ruth Ann, but there it was, a cold hard fact. Margie had fallen in love with a girl, who could substitute for what she couldn't have.

Ruth Ann must have seen the look on Margie's face, because she saved the day. "I don't think she looks at all like me. She's much prettier."

Margie saw Amy blush under the weight of Ruth Ann's stare. She began to feel better, because Ruth Ann was having the same effect on Amy that she had on everyone, it seemed. Amy was smitten. There was something so alluring about Ruth Ann. It drove both gay and straight women to her like ants to a picnic. Margie had witnessed it on the beach when they were surfing. The men just drooled, but Ruth Ann was definitely in her element around women. Margie thought she now understood the term bedroom eyes. This woman could talk the clothes off a nun with a wink and a grin. Ruth Ann was the embodiment of southern charm and charisma. Combined with her innate animal magnetism she was impossible to resist, at least she was to the women with whom Margie had observed her. Even the post office lady got dreamy eyed when she talked about Ruth Ann.

Amy managed, finally, to stutter out, "Tha...Thank you."

There was an awkward moment, where Ruth Ann and Margie just stared at each other. Margie could have sworn she saw something in Ruth Ann's eyes, she had never seen before. She was looking at Margie like a woman, not a child, and then she caught herself. Ruth Ann pulled her gaze from Margie's and craned her neck to see over the dunes.

"I can't wait to get out there. How are the waves?"

"Pretty good," Margie answered casually, but her head was still trying to wrap itself around that look a moment ago.

Linda opened the passenger side door of the car. "Well, since you're here, you can help us carry in all this stuff. Miss Writer there doesn't go anywhere without all her accoutrements. That old typewriter weighs a ton."

The four of them moved everything from the car into the tiny cottage. It was more of an efficiency than a cottage, but it did have a deck that looked out over the ocean. When everything was out of the car, Margie figured they should leave Ruth Ann and Linda alone. After all, they hadn't seen each other in months. Ruth Ann had said she picked Linda up at the Norfolk airport that morning.

"Well, we'll go and let you two relax. I'm sure it's been a long day for both of you." Margie was pleased at how mature she sounded.

She grabbed Amy's hand and led her to the door. Amy had been nearly comatose the entire time they were in Ruth Ann's presence. She had hardly said two words, other than, "Where should I put this?"

Ruth Ann followed them out on the deck. "Hey, can you two get away for a dinner with us, tonight? We'll cook steaks on the grill."

Margie would most definitely be there. She wasn't sure about Amy at this point. She might have to dunk her in the ocean to wake her up from the stunned state she seemed stuck in. Though she stood right there, Amy didn't appear to be in the room mentally.

"We'll be here." Margie spoke for Amy. "What time?"

Ruth Ann turned to Linda, "About eight okay with you?"

Linda did not look pleased, but she used her TV background to cover her disappointment with a fake smile. Margie noticed it. Ruth Ann did, too. Margie saw Ruth Ann narrow her eyes at Linda, who then responded, "Oh, sure. That will be fine."

"See you later, then," Margie said, pushing Amy out the door in front of her. She could sense the mood had changed in the room and she wanted out.

Ruth Ann stopped Margie, by grabbing her elbow, just as she stepped through the threshold to the deck outside, "It's really good to see you again."

Margie smiled at her hero, friend, her obsession. "Yeah, it's good to see you, too."

Another twitch of the iris. Margie saw it clearly this time. Ruth Ann was wrestling demons. Margie was sure it had nothing to do with her. She wasn't going to read anything into this that really wasn't there. Something was going down, but Margie wasn't sure what it was. She left with Amy and headed back to the office to retrieve her bike. Then she and Amy walked back toward the lighthouse, barely speaking, each lost in thoughts of their own.

#

Ida had gone to her brother's house for the weekend, leaving Margie in the care of her father. Even at sixteen, Margie still couldn't get her mother to leave her alone at home. If she didn't smoother before she turned eighteen, it would be a miracle. Her dad let her do as she pleased, for the most part. He trusted her to do the right thing and she almost always did. He forgave her youthful transgressions and missteps much more easily than Ida did. All he had to know was where he could locate her if he needed to. She would have lied to Ida, but for his trust, she owed her father the truth.

"Dad, I've been invited to a cookout at the Outer Banks Cottages. That woman I taught to surf last year is back. She asked Amy and me to come eat with them, tonight."

He answered from his usual place in front of the TV, "That lady that gave you the stationary?"

"Yes, sir," she answered from the top of the stairs, having already zoomed past him.

"She seems nice. Take her a watermelon, if you want. I put two in the garage refrigerator."

"Does that mean I can drive?"

Margie hopped back down the stairs two at a time and swung on the doorjamb, propelling her body to land flatfooted, facing her father. This behavior was strictly forbidden if Ida was in the house. She was constantly complaining about Margie's fingerprints on the doors frames and ceilings. Margie couldn't help it. Sometimes she just couldn't contain all that energy.

Her father smiled up at her. "Your mother doesn't like that."

"I know. Can I drive?" Margie cut right to the chase. Her father could not resist her dimples and she knew it. She poured on the charm. "Ida will never know."

"You're going to get us both in trouble," her father answered, but he was pulling the keys to his truck out of his pocket. "Be home by midnight, and if I come lookin' my truck better be parked at that motel."

It was an idle threat. He'd be asleep in an hour, two at the most. Besides he wouldn't have any way to get there. Margie would have his truck.

"I'll be there. I'm going to pick up Amy and drop her back off. Other than that, I'll be at the motel."

"Okay, sweetheart. Be careful."

Margie leaned down and kissed her father on the cheek. "Thanks, Dad. I will."

She ran back upstairs. First, she had to call Amy and tell her the good news and then she had to shower and change. She achieved more than her goal, which was to get to the motel tonight and she had done it without telling a lie. She hadn't exactly told all the truth of it, but she had not lied. Margie led her father on a bit, true, but he was making assumptions, and that she could not help. She would tell him the whole truth one day. He wouldn't be happy, but he would love her just the same. Of that, she was sure.

She dialed Amy's number from her parents' phone in the master bedroom. They had walked to the lighthouse, where Margie left Amy to gather her things and catch a ride home with Debbie. Margie had ridden her bike home. They hadn't really said two words to each other the entire way.

Just before they parted ways, Margie asked, "Is there something you need to tell me, Amy?"

Amy looked away. Margie thought she saw tears in her eyes. After a moment, Amy said, "We can talk later. Let's just enjoy the dinner."

That made Margie joyously happy. She didn't want to deal with relationship problems with Ruth Ann here. If it was serious, she would be torn between taking the time to fix it, and spending every moment that she could with Ruth Ann. In her heart, she knew Ruth Ann would win out and that decision would lead to bigger problems. Amy just needed to understand and chill out for two weeks. Then everything would go back to normal.

Amy picked up on the third ring. Margie could hear little kids playing loudly in the background. Amy said, "Hello."

"Hey, it's me. Dad's letting me drive the truck. Pick you up at seven forty-five, okay?"

"You have the truck? Till when?" Amy was shocked.

Margie answered proudly, "Until midnight."

"Your mom's going to kill your dad, if she finds out, and you'll be next on the list." Amy had been around long enough to know Ida pretty well.

"She's not going to know, unless you blab," Margie said, trying to sound playful, but meaning it.

"I sure as hell won't be the one to tell her. Pick me up at the end of the road so my mom won't see the truck. That way she can't blab either, and don't stop anywhere. This village is like Peyton Place. Somebody would tell your mom they saw you."

Margie laughed. She had trained Amy well. "I'll be careful. Besides, she'll scream at Bob more than me, on this one. I can hear her now, 'You're the adult, Bob!'" Amy laughed. It felt good to hear her laugh. She'd been so down lately. Margie added, "I love it when you laugh, Amy. I'll see you in a few."

Margie hung up thinking how much she really did love Amy. They were young, like Ruth Ann said, but they had such a connection. Margie couldn't imagine Amy not being in her life. They were destined, if not to spend the rest of their lives together, to remain a part of one another forever. Amy was her best friend and sometimes lover. They weren't sex crazed. Well, they were, but they tried to keep it in check. They may have not been fooling around with boys, but they were definitely having sex. The moral standards of the day required they at least feel guilty about it and try not to do it too much.

#

Margie was a relatively experienced driver for only having a license for a week. She had been driving on the beach since she could reach the pedals and before that from her father's lap. She got her permit when she turned fifteen and had driven Ida back and forth to Wilson numerous times. Still this first outing alone was thrilling.

Margie picked up Amy right on time. She lumbered up in the big four-wheel drive. Amy had to hop to get in it. She was wearing the perfume that drove Margie wild, Opium. Margie thought the name appropriate, because it was like a drug to her. She could already feel the heat rising around her neck. Amy looked fantastic. She was wearing the cut off jeans that had the same effect on Margie as the perfume, and a white sleeveless blouse that Margie was already fantasizing about unbuttoning slowly. Amy was smiling. Not showing any signs of the moping girl she had been for the last few days.

"You look beautiful," Margie said, once Amy was inside the truck. She dared not kiss her, but she desperately wanted to. Instead she reached across the truck's bench seat and squeezed Amy's hand.

"So do you," was Amy's reply, as she returned Margie's smile.

Margie wore a pair of white tennis shorts and a blue Lacoste polo shirt. She was even wearing shoes, tennis shoes, but still her feet were covered. The white socks and white shorts made her darkly tanned legs stand out even more. The blue shirt exactly matched the color of her eyes. From the expression on Amy's face, Margie thought she had done a good job choosing the outfit.

"Thank you," she said, and put the truck in gear.

When they reached the turn at the end of the sandy lane, Margie stopped the truck before pulling onto Flower Ridge Road. She looked in all the mirrors and around the truck. Not seeing anyone, she reached across the seat and pulled Amy to her. Margie kissed Amy, trying to hold back the passion that cried for her to rip off Amy's clothes right there.

Amy pushed Margie away. "Are you nuts? Somebody is going to see us."

Margie tried to kiss Amy again, saying, "I don't care."

"Well, I do," Amy said, sliding back across the seat and out of Margie's reach. "Ida's off the island and you've lost your mind."

Margie grinned at Amy. She was so cute when she was flustered. She winked at her. "Later, then?"

Amy grinned back, coyly, "Maybe, if you're good."

Margie put the truck back in gear and they rolled off slowly, while she said, "If that's not what you wanted, why did you wear that perfume?"

"We're having dinner with your fantasy woman. I needed something to keep your attention."

Margie's eyebrows shot up. "My fantasy woman?"

"Yeah, you know the one person in the world that could knock on your door and say, 'Hey, come on,' and you'd go with no questions asked."

"You really think I would do that. Geeze, she's eleven years older than me."

"Margie Whooten, you would sleep with her in a heartbeat."

"Well, you were quite taken with her yourself," Margie shot back.

Amy turned in the seat and leaned against the door. She contemplated what Margie said and then offered, "I've been thinking about that. It's her eyes, don't you think? It's like behind them she hides the keys to the kingdom. When she looked at me, it almost took the air from my lungs, but it wasn't sexual, it was awe. Awe at how gorgeous she is, and how charming and sweet she seemed. It's more than looks though. It's some kind of woman attracting pheromone. That girlfriend of hers is no slouch either."

Margie winked at Amy. "Neither are you."

They arrived at the motel a few minutes later. The twilight sky cast a soft, gray-blue glow over the sand, highlighting the tips of the frothy surf in the distance. The moon was just rising and would be full at its zenith this evening. The amber glow from the cottage windows caught Ruth Ann silhouetted at the corner of the deck, her eyes cast out over the beach.

She heard Margie and Amy approaching and turned to greet them, steak tongs in one hand, a huge grin engulfing her face. "You two clean up very nicely. Come on up. Would you like a coke?"

"Yes, thank you," Amy said, sounding coherent in Ruth Ann's presence for the first time.

"Sure. Hey, where can I put this?" Margie offered up the watermelon she carried from the truck.

Ruth Ann reached in the cooler beside the grill, fishing out two Cokes. She handed them to the girls and took the watermelon from Margie. "Thanks. We'll have this for desert. The steaks are almost ready."

Margie relaxed. Amy had gotten over whatever it was that upset her earlier and apparently was planning to enjoy the evening. They were having dinner together with two other women who wouldn't care if they smiled at each other, held hands, or even kissed. It was the first time Margie felt comfortable in her own skin. She could just be herself. She didn't have to pretend to be what she knew in her heart she wasn't.

Dinner inside the little cottage was intimate and went well. The conversation rambled from Anita Bryant to the books Margie read over the last year. They lapsed into serious political discussion, heads leaned in close together, soon to find themselves laughing hysterically, as Amy or Margie told stories of their high school escapades.

If Margie could have stopped time she would have frozen it there, shutting the world out, escaping forever into this moment when she first felt it. It enveloped her senses like a low crawling fog from the floor, swirling and climbing up her body, until the headiness of it intoxicated her. The overwhelming energy of women pulled at her, called her out, told her she was one of them and it was going to be a glorious life.

Ida always said, "You never fly so high that you don't have to come back down." In the moments after dinner those words would ring in Margie's ears. Once the table was cleaned of dishes, the four of them went out on the deck to relax. Ruth Ann and Linda had been drinking wine with the meal, but Ruth Ann switched to a soft drink when they got outside. Linda opened another bottle of wine, already beginning to show the effects of the first one. There had been signs of tension between the two older women all night, but it had not dampened the mood. That all changed rather quickly.

The deck was small with only enough room for two chairs on one side and the grill on the other. Ruth Ann and Margie stood leaning on the deck railing while Amy and Linda sat in the chairs, each pair involved in their own conversations. Ruth Ann and Margie were talking about surfing and setting up a schedule for the next few days. Tomorrow was supposed to be stormy, but the rest of the week looked great.

Linda interrupted the conversation at the deck railing, asking, "Hey, Ruth Ann. Amy here wants to know how long distance relationships work out. Should I tell her the truth?"

"Truth" hung in the air like a smoke ring, lilting and flowing into the shape of the slight slur now evident in Linda's speech.

Ruth Ann stiffened. Margie watched the smile slide off Ruth Ann's face, her dark eyes glaring at Linda. Margie waited for Ruth Ann's reply, but none came. The muscles in Ruth Ann's jaw twitched, as she clenched her teeth, but she remained silent.

Linda, however, was just getting started. "What? The great lesbian writer has no comment. Don't you have answers for these darling children who worship you, oh wise one?"

Ruth Ann spoke this time. It was a low, calm, but very stern voice that said, "I believe you may have mistakenly had a bit too much to drink. If you like, I can dismiss our guests, which would be rude, or you can do the polite thing and excuse yourself."

Margie looked at Amy, who was wide-eyed at the exchange. She offered to the seething Ruth Ann, "Maybe we should just go."

"No, stay," Linda said, "you should know a little bit more about your hero there. She's not what you think she is, Margie. She's just like all the rest. Nothing special about her."

"Linda, they don't need to take part in this. Leave them alone, they're just kids."

"All the more reason for them not to worship at a false prophet's feet, don't you think?" Linda turned back to Amy, not giving Ruth Ann time to respond, "You see, when women like Ruth Ann are left alone, they can't be trusted. They leave a trail of broken hearts strewn along this path of infidelity. Long distance relationships to them mean, what you don't see won't hurt you. The problem is you do see it, but you're not supposed to say anything."

Margie saw that Amy was beginning to cry. She wanted to belt Linda for causing it. She knelt on one knee in front of Amy. "Hey, don't cry. I'm not like that, besides we see each other every day."

Ruth Ann, livid, stepped up to Linda. "That was asinine and uncalled for. Go inside before you continue to embarrass me and yourself."

At that exact moment, Margie's whole world crumbled. Amy burst into tears, crying out, "We're moving to Alaska next weekend!"

Margie froze. Everything around her stopped. There was no sound, no movement. Not even her heart was beating. During that pause in the elements, memories of Amy flashed through her mind. The first time she saw her, the first time they shared a kiss, the first time they said "I love you," all of it flew by in a flash of color and spent emotions. It rocked her hard. So hard that when the world started moving again, she fell off her knee, landing on the deck with a thud.

"Oh shit!" It was Ruth Ann speaking. Suddenly she was standing over the two of them. "Hey, shhh, shhh," she said, patting the backs of the now despondent teenagers. "It's going to be okay. Shhh..." She looked over at Margie, who was clutching her knees to her chest, not crying, not saying anything. "Hey, you okay?" She got no response. "Margie, are you okay?"

Margie snapped out of her misery long enough to nod. Amy must have held that secret in for the last few weeks. That would explain her mood. What Margie interpreted as jealousy of her relationship with Ruth Ann had been a heartbreaking secret. How had she held it in this long? Margie was devastated, but she knew she needed to take care of Amy. She untangled her lanky body. Standing over her, Margie reached down, gently pushing the hair away from Amy's tear streaked face.

"Amy, come on, let's go." She stuck out her hand for Amy to take, which she did, slowly rising out of the chair. Margie paused in front of Ruth Ann. "I'll talk to you tomorrow."

Ruth Ann touched Margie's shoulder, giving her a tender squeeze. "You've got more important things to deal with. I'll see you when I see you, okay."

"Sure," Margie replied weakly.

Ruth Ann gave another short squeeze to Margie's shoulder. "You know where I am. Anytime, day or night, you come if you need me."

Margie nodded acceptance of the invitation and moved off toward the steps. Linda, standing now, said, "I'm sorry, Margie."

For the very first time in her life, Margie was truly disrespectful to an adult. With a voice absolutely dripping with disdain, Margie said, "Fuck you, Linda."

#

"It's 9:00 pm and still 82 degrees with a heat index that make it feel like 92 on the Outer Banks. Try to stay cool our there. We lead off this hour with the number one song this week, Undercover Angel by Alan O'Day."

#

In the dunes, on an isolated stretch of beach, the two young lovers clung to each other for dear life. Passions spent and tears dried, they lay together looking up at the stars. There was nothing Margie could do. They had talked out all the options.

A week had gone by since Amy told Margie she was moving. Since then they had tried everything imaginable to stay together. Amy's mother wouldn't let her live with Margie until they graduated, even though Ida said she could. Ida must have realized how devastated the two of them were and had been surprisingly accommodating this past week, while Margie spent every waking moment, and most sleeping ones too, by

Amy's side. To the adults the girls were merely reacting to losing a best friend. None of them could fathom the actual depth of that loss.

This was their last night together. Margie had only seen Ruth Ann twice. She went by the morning after the bomb was dropped about the move. Ruth Ann understood that Margie had to spend time with Amy. Later in the week, Ruth Ann took them to lunch, as sort of an apology for the way the evening at the cottage had gone. Linda went back to Chicago after only staying a few days. As far as Margie could tell, that relationship was over, but she hadn't asked. She was more concerned with her own heartbreak at the moment.

Outside the restaurant, Ruth Ann gave Amy a card with her phone number and address on it.

"You call me, if you just need to talk." Ruth Ann paused and looked from Amy to Margie. "Look, I know this feels like the end of the world, but two years isn't really as long as you think. Then you'll be in college and you can be a bit more flexible about where you choose to live. If you're supposed to be together, you will be. You have to believe that."

Those words rang hollow now, with only hours left before Amy would be gone. Margie fought back against another wave of tears. It was no use. She never dreamed of pain like this. The hot tears ran down the sides of her face and into her hair. She rolled over and pulled Amy up close to her side, where she could see into those brown eyes, the ones currently filled with tears.

"I swear, one way or another, we're going to be together. I'm going to love you forever, Amy, I promise."

Broken hearts and broken promises always begin with the best of intentions.

#

Saturday night found Margie seated beside Ruth Ann on the steps of the motel cottage. Margie had seen Amy off that morning with tears streaming down both their faces. She drove back to her house, crawled into bed, and slept until dark. Ida checked on her once and was met with a surly "Go away!" After Margie awoke, she asked her dad if she could borrow his truck. He looked at her with understanding and silently handed her the keys. Ida started to protest, but Bob put his hand up to quiet her.

"Go on, honey," he said, "Just be home around midnight."

Margie drove straight to the motel and found Ruth Ann pecking away at the typewriter. She stopped writing and came out on the deck to sit with Margie. They sat for a long time, not talking. Margie was tired of crying.

She wanted to be able to talk without tears, so she waited for the ache to subside a bit in Ruth Ann's calming presence.

When she was ready, Margie asked, in a voice raspy with emotion, "How long is it going to hurt like this?"

Ruth Ann put her arm around Margie's shoulder, letting the younger woman lean against her. "It depends on you. If you let yourself wallow in your misery, it will take a lot longer."

"What am I supposed to do, just forget about her?"

"No, that's not what I'm saying at all. I know it's hard, but let's look at this rationally. You aren't likely to see Amy again until next summer, if then. A lot can change in a year. There is no sense in wasting a lot of energy worrying over something that far in the future, especially because you have no control over it. You can control how you go about your life in the here and now."

Margie pulled away from Ruth Ann, snapping at her, "She's coming back!"

"I hope she does. I really do." Ruth Ann paused, before she said, "But, who did she fall in love with, a moping, depressed girl or happy, go-lucky Margie? Don't let this change you. I've seen this thing called love take down some very strong women—"

"But not you," Margie interrupted. She was wounded and she attacked the only person within striking distance. "You seem to be the one taking people down. What did Linda mean about you not being who I thought you were? What did you do, cheat on her?"

To Margie's amazement, Ruth Ann did not reply angrily. She calmly answered. "Linda misunderstood the nature of our relationship. What I did when she was not around was no concern of hers. I gave her one hundred percent of what I had to give her. Those other women didn't detract from what I felt for her."

"You didn't love her," Margie spat.

"Why do you say that?"

Margie's anger was growing and she wasn't sure why she was taking it out on Ruth Ann, but she continued, "Because if you loved her, she would have been enough."

Ruth Ann became defensive. "I don't expect you to understand."

"Why, because I'm sixteen? I know a cheater trying to justify her actions when I see one. I don't need a college degree for that."

Ruth Ann tilted her head to one side and raised an eyebrow. A grin crept into the corners of her mouth. "No, I guess you don't." She paused a second, before continuing, "Margie, long distance relationships built on the quicksand of youthful affairs are not the romantic ideal people try to make them out to be. The letters and phone calls that you live for in the beginning become less frequent. The time you have together is short and rarely fulfilling, and you change in the other person's absence, as do they. Maybe you and Amy will be the exception, but just prepare yourself if you aren't."

Margie stood up. Even though part of her brain knew Ruth Ann was making sense, she didn't want to hear it. "I'm not like you. If I tell someone I love them, then I mean it. You try to play yourself off as some innocent bystander, while you break Linda's heart. You're full of shit Ruth Ann."

Margie tore down the steps and ran to her father's truck. Hot tears streamed down her face. She looked up to see Ruth Ann standing in front of the truck. Margie glared at her through the glass and cranked the engine. She yanked the truck into reverse, jammed on the gas, and threw sand and gravel in Ruth Ann's general direction for a brief but satisfying three seconds. She slammed the truck into drive and drove out of the parking lot, not looking back.

#

Tuesday morning Margie woke with a start. Her mind flashed on Ruth Ann standing in front of the truck. Calmed considerably and suddenly stricken with the knowledge that she had probably alienated the only real friend she had left, Margie dressed quickly and caught a ride with her dad to the lighthouse. He always got up early and drove down to the Red Drum Tackle Shop to chat with the boys.

The weather on Sunday and Monday had been drizzly all day. Margie had not left the house. In fact, she spent very little time out of bed. She wallowed in her misery to the point that Ida thought she was sick and wanted to take her to the doctor. Her dad had finally persuaded Ida to leave Margie alone. When she exited the truck at the lighthouse, he got out with her. He leaned on the back of the truck across from Margie, while she grabbed her surfboard out of the back.

He cleared his throat. A sign Margie knew as his "listen to me" signal. "Margie, I know you've lost your best friend and I do believe it hurts. I'm going to give you some time to get yourself together, but in a few days, you have to go back to your workouts. I think the focus will help take your mind off your troubles."

"Sure, Dad. Just give me till the end of the week. I'll be all right in a few days."

"I love ya', Margie."

"I love you, too, Dad. Thanks for keeping Mom off my back."

"Well, I can't hold her off forever, so you better start acting a little more like yourself at home."

"Yeah, okay. Hey, I'm going down to the motel to see if that lady still wants her lessons. I kinda blew her off when I found out Amy was leaving. I'll be home later this afternoon, probably around five, okay?"

"That'll be fine. You be careful." He climbed back in the truck and drove away.

Margie ran the half a mile up the beach, carrying the surfboard with her. She was breathless, but relieved when she saw that Ruth Ann's car was still in the parking lot. The door was closed on the cottage and there didn't appear to be any movement inside. Margie leaned the surfboard against the deck and climbed up the steps. She decided to sit and wait until Ruth Ann came out the door. It gave her time to think about what she was going to say.

Margie was sorry she had taken her frustration and anger out on Ruth Ann. It really wasn't her place to judge Ruth Ann's treatment of Linda. She barely knew Linda and wasn't privy to the inner workings of their relationship. Maybe Ruth Ann had made it clear that Linda wasn't the only woman with whom she was involved. It could be that Linda expected too much. She wondered if it hurt Ruth Ann that Linda left.

Her answer came in the form of a long legged blonde walking out the cottage door with Ruth Ann. The woman froze when she saw Margie. It was barely eight o'clock in the morning and Margie was sure this woman was trying to leave Ruth Ann's without being seen. Too late. Margie recognized her right away. It was a girl she'd known all her life. She was six years older and had been away at college most of the last four years. She in turn recognized Margie and flushed blood red.

Ruth Ann smiled at Margie. "I take it you two know each other?"

Margie smiled back, because it looked like Ruth Ann wasn't mad at her. She nodded at the girl. "Yeah, Susie and I have known each other a long time."

Susie said, "Hello, Margie. It's been awhile. You've grown up."

Ruth Ann chuckled. "You have no idea."

Susie looked shocked. Misinterpreting what Ruth Ann had said, she asked her, "Are you sleeping with this girl, too?"

Margie and Ruth Ann replied at the same time, "No," which caused them both to laugh.

Ruth Ann added, "She's just a friend and my surfing coach. She's cool. She won't say anything."

Susie looked at Margie. "My parents don't know. I'd like to keep it that way."

Margie laughed. "My parents don't know either, and I'd very much like to keep it that way. You know Ida. She'd kill me."

"Your secret is safe with me, hon'. I didn't know you were—" Susie stuttered.

"Yes, Susie, I am, but like I said, I'd like to keep that from folks around here for the time being."

"I hear you," Susie said.

"This never happened," Margie said, waving her hand at Ruth Ann and Susie.

"Now that we have that settled, Susie was just leaving," Ruth Ann said, "and I believe I have a surfing lesson to get ready for."

Susie left and Margie went inside the cottage with Ruth Ann while she got dressed. Margie sat on the couch while Ruth Ann went into the bedroom. She didn't close the door all the way, so Margie could hear her speaking.

"So, you've decided that even though I'm full of shit, you'd still like to be my friend," Ruth Ann called from the bedroom. "I have to admit, you figured it out quicker than most."

"I don't have the right to judge you, that's all," Margie answered. "I don't know what kind of arrangement you and Linda had."

"Whatever the arrangement was, it's clear I didn't communicate my part of it very well." Ruth Ann laughed.

Margie saw Ruth Ann flash by the mirror on the wall in the bedroom, visible through the slightly opened door. She jerked her eyes away and focused on the floor at her feet. Ruth Ann was naked on the other side of that door. Margie could not fight the urge to look again. When she did she saw Ruth Ann bending down to put on her swimsuit bottoms. Margie swallowed hard. At that very moment, Ruth Ann's head popped up and she saw Margie in the mirror. Margie was glued to the couch, yet every muscle and nerve was screaming, "Run!" Ruth Ann grinned and winked. She reached up and shut the door a little more and never said a word about it.

To Margie's relief, Ruth Ann asked, "So, how are the waves this morning?"

They spent the rest of the time it took for Ruth Ann to get dressed talking about the surf and the weather. They picked up where they left off as friends, spending the remainder of the week in each other's company whenever Margie could get away. They surfed and played tennis. Ruth Ann was good and taught Margie the overhead serve. She was sorry she had, because Margie corrected her swing quickly and started to ace Ruth

Ann quite often. Margie went back to being her old self around the house and both of her parents seemed relieved.

Although she still thought of Amy frequently, the stabbing pain had eased some. She could now go a whole day without tears. Margie was learning how to control her emotions. She was beginning the process of adulthood, when a person learned how to erect walls around those deep places she wanted no one ever to enter. Her first broken heart had taught her one thing. Don't ever love something too much.

On their last night together, Ruth Ann and Margie talked about that very subject. They were sitting on the deck, Saturday night, watching the stars in the moonless sky. Margie hadn't mentioned the night she told Ruth Ann she was full of shit, but she had thought long and hard about what Ruth Ann had said.

Margie spoke after a pause in conversation, "The other night when you were telling me about long distance relationships—"

Ruth Ann cut her off, "Margie, I shouldn't have laid all that on you. I should have just held you and let you cry. I don't know, I guess I was trying to save you future heartache. It wasn't what you needed at the moment."

"It's okay. I understand why you did it," Margie said. "I just wasn't in the mood to hear it."

Ruth Ann laughed. "I got that message loud and clear."

"Sorry," Margie said, but she was grinning.

Ruth Ann focused her brown eyes on her young companion. Whenever she did this Margie felt drawn in, swept away by the sheer intensity of that stare. She felt herself take a deep breath and tried to let it out slowly. Margie didn't want Ruth Ann to know how unnerving she could be at times.

"Margie, if there is one piece of advice I could give you it would be that you have to be careful with women. What I mean is most women, not all but most, tend to fall in love quickly and hard. Too often sex is equated with love. There isn't a lot of dating in the lesbian world. Women meet, they sleep together, and suddenly they are sharing a house. They rarely take the time to find out who the other woman is until they're already in the relationship. Sometimes it works out great. The two women really get along and genuinely like each other, but nine times out of ten it ends in one person being invested in the relationship, while the other is desperately trying to get away."

"You bailed out," Margie said.

Ruth Ann looked puzzled.

"It's what we say in surfing," Margie explained, "when you dive off your board before you wipeout. No need to ride a wave, if it isn't going to turn out well."

"You are way too wise for your age."

"It's all the books I've been reading." Margie grinned and then asked, "Don't you want a permanent relationship?"

"Not now. I'm young and having the time of my life. I'm traveling all over the country. Why shouldn't I experience everything that's offered to me?"

Margie laughed. "So, what you're saying is you have women throwing themselves at you everywhere you go."

Ruth Ann cast a wicked grin in Margie's direction. "Yeah, kinda, but that's not all of it. I'm meeting people who have made a difference in how women are perceived in the world. I'm teaching women who are going to make a difference in how we are seen in the future. I just want to be open to experience it all, not tied down to someone who needs to know where I am and who I'm with all the time. If I wanted that, I'd date men."

"Amy was getting like that. It drove me nuts," Margie said, realizing only then that she and Amy had been on a crash course to disaster, before she found out Amy was moving.

"You're young, Margie. Enjoy it. Meet lots of people. Go places. Live your life, before you tie yourself down."

Margie thought about that statement for a moment. Then she asked Ruth Ann, "Do you think you'll ever settle down?"

"When the right one comes along, I guess I'll know and yes, I would settle down then. I'm only twenty-seven. Give me a few years before that happens."

"So many women, so little time," Margie said, laughing.

"You know you're one smartass kid." Ruth Ann joined Margie in laughter.

When the laughter subsided, Margie said, "So, you're leaving in the morning. I guess we're back to writing letters. I wish I had spent more time with you."

"You had other things to deal with. It's understandable," Ruth Ann said. "I'm going to give you my phone number. You can call me collect any time. I'd like to hear your voice occasionally."

Margie brightened. The chance to talk to Ruth Ann, not just in letters, was more than she could have hoped. She covered her excitement with, "I'd give you mine, but Ida would sniff you out in a second."

Ruth Ann smiled. "Yeah, I know. My mom was like that, too. Do you get the twenty questions every time you meet someone new? You know, 'Who are her parents? What do they do for a living?' That kind of thing."

"Oh yeah, every time. I don't care how much money people have or where they came from, but it sure matters to Ida."

Ruth Ann nodded in agreement. "I don't know why our mothers are like that. It appears to me they are afraid of people different from them. Now that I'm out to my family, I thought it would change, but she still wants to know all about the women with whom I'm involved. I suppose I'm to find a debutante to keep up the family standards."

"Do you think Ida will ever accept me for who I am?" Margie asked, sincerely hoping Ruth Ann would have the answer.

"She will eventually. At least, I think so. You know her better than I do, but most mothers get over it after some time to think. It won't be easy. She'll hurt you first, because she's hurt. Our mothers have high hopes for us. In their minds, only a man and a white picket fence will ensure our happy futures. That's the Cinderella dream they have for us. You have to give her time to let that dream die."

"I've come close to screaming, 'I'm a lesbian,' at her, when she was ranting over my clothes or playing ball. She really wanted a frilly girl and she got me. I guess that's enough disappointment for her at the moment. I think I'll hold off on the announcement till I'm in college. At least I won't have to live with her while she freaks out."

Ruth Ann smiled knowingly. "Hon, you need to hold off on that announcement as long as possible, trust me. Keep it to yourself for a while. You might change your mind and then you'd be stuck with the label."

Margie laughed loudly. "I won't be changing my mind. I don't like guys that way. They're not appealing to me, but now, a pretty girl turns my head." She paused, thinking, and then added, "Have you been with a guy like that?"

"Yes, I had a steady boyfriend for years, before I made up my mind to be true to what I was really feeling. You read the book. It was in there."

"I didn't know what was true and what was made up," Margie said.

"Not much, really. It's all true in one way or another," Ruth Ann looked out over the water.

"So you're mom really slapped you and threw you out of the house?"

"Yep, she cut me off. Wouldn't even let Dad pay my senior year tuition. I was lucky to find scholarships to help me. That's why I wrote the book. I was so mad I had to get it out of my system, but when I started writing it, I had a chance to try and see it from her perspective. I found the humor in the situation. That book was a catharsis for me. I grew up a lot writing it."

"Well, when I tell Ida I'm sure there will be hell to pay. I'm glad I'll be on scholarship, so I don't have to depend on her."

"That's another thing, too. Don't come out before you sign with a school and even then keep it quiet. They don't cotton too well to professed lesbians in the sports world, yet. I don't care how good you are. If they find out you're a lesbian and open about it, they'll find a way to get rid of you."

"I hadn't thought about that," Margie said, suddenly stricken with fear of being found out.

"Everybody always says, if we all came out the world would see how many of us there are and get over their prejudices, but that's not true. Intolerance is not easily overcome. Look at the civil rights movement. The laws are in place, but the bigotry still exists, even if you don't see it."

"Come on, you're not one of those, 'I am woman, hear me roar,' chicks are you? I've read the constitution. They meant 'man' to mean humanity, not the male gender. My rights are guaranteed. My take is that I just have to make sure those rights aren't violated, but I'm not a man hating feminist."

"Most feminists are not man-haters, nor lesbians for that matter, but there are exceptions to every rule. Those are the ones portrayed in the media. The 'feminist agenda,' as they like to call it, is not to diminish male roles in society. I think what we really want is to work side by side with men, but as equals, not subordinates. We want to be valued for our worth."

"Can't you do more by showing than telling? I mean, why don't we just do what we want and show people that women can do anything, if they set their minds to it?" Margie asked.

"You're a smart kid, Margie, but you've been sheltered. For example, you're a surfer. Do the guys around here give you a hard time?"

Margie's brow creased, not knowing where this was going. She answered. "No, most of them taught me how to surf. They're cool."

"Well, it's not cool other places. Out in California, the guys have at times refused to leave the surf during the women's competition. The girls have to surf around them, while they try to get in the way. Just last year, the President of the Women's International Surfing Association was sexually assaulted by male surfers at a party. They didn't like her moaning about the treatment women were getting. She doesn't surf now. She fled to New York."

This scared Margie. She said the only thing she could think of. "Was it because she was talking or because she's a lesbian?"

"She isn't a lesbian, but would it have mattered? She was a woman the old boys needed to put in her place."

"I guess I am sheltered. I mean I read a lot, but you don't see things like that in the paper. If you do, they don't tell you the whole story."

Ruth Ann agreed, "You're right. They don't usually tell you the woman got what was coming to her, but they hint at it. What you say is true. We do have the same rights as men. We just have to make sure everyone knows it. You keep doing what you're doing. Ignore the barriers. Women like you will change this government. You'll see."

"Do you think there will ever be a time when lesbians don't have to hide?"

"One day, maybe, but we have thousands of years of homophobia to contend with. It's going to take some time."

Margie glanced at her watch. "Damn, I have to go. I have to get Dad's truck home before midnight."

Ruth Ann stood up. "Well, I guess this is it. I'm leaving before sunup. I have to be in Chapel Hill before noon tomorrow."

"Well, I guess I'll see you in your letters."

Ruth Ann pulled Margie in for a tight hug. "We're friends forever, Margie Whooten. I'll see you when I see you."

Chapter Four

*"On Billboards national singles chart, the best selling
song in the U. S. A for the third week in a row, here's
'I Just Want To Be Your Everything,' Andy Gibb"*
American top 40, Broadcast August 13, 1977

"Hey!"

Margie jogged down the bank, paralleling the little sunfish sailboat.

"Hey!" She yelled a bit louder that time

Still no response from the boat. Up ahead, a long pier ran perpendicular to the sailboat's path. If she could get to the end quickly enough, Margie might be able to avert a minor disaster. Well, how major or minor was yet to be determined.

Margie picked up speed, dodging curious campers and leaping over obstacles in her path. She turned at the base of the pier, skidding past it and then recovering for the push to the end.

"Hey, Val! Hey! Watch out!"

Clipping along at a pretty good pace, the young sailor was getting the most out of the sunfish's small sail area. With the wind at her back, the captain filled the sails and pulled taught the line. Keeping the sail filled and the hull barely touching the surface, they were the fastest vessel on Queen Creek. Under different circumstances, Margie would have admired the thirteen-year-old skipper's skill.

Valerie Duke, the camp's head lifeguard, leaned back against the sunfish's mast, her legs stretched out on the deck. The speeding craft's skillful young skipper had a major crush on the Wonder Woman look alike. There were very few at the camp who had not fallen under Val's spell. Margie was no different than the girl at the helm of the little sailboat.

She had arrived three weeks ago, as a substitute for the head lifeguard who had to leave suddenly. Valerie, who was only eighteen and starting college in the fall, moved up in rank and Margie took her place. When one of Bob's old coaching buddies called in need of a lifeguard, her parents thought this time away from home would be just the thing to drive away the cloud of Amy's leaving. What they didn't know was that Margie had seen Bob's buddy only once, on the day she arrived. Other than that, Margie was being treated like a young adult, with all the freedoms that come with it. She just thought it was cool to be paid to stay near Val.

"I don't think she knows she has a crush on you," Greg said, after finding out the kid, smitten to the point of recklessness, had summoned the courage to ask Val to go sailing with her.

Greg, Val's boyfriend, claimed alpha male status among the camp's counseling staff. He was in charge of the canoes and sailboats, conveniently located just beyond the swimming area where Val ruled the waves from the high chair. Late at night, after the campers from all over North Carolina were tucked away in cabins with their adult chaperones, Greg and Val held court like royals, as the counselors came out to play. Margie was the youngest of the group. It had been an educational experience, and not what Ida and Bob had in mind when they mutually agreed this was a good idea.

"If I go sailing with her, maybe she'll stop being a little stalker," Val answered. "She asks me every day. What do you think, Margie?"

Margie didn't think the two lovebirds noticed she was there, much less wanted her opinion. Caught off guard, she answered without thinking, "She's a harmless kid with a crush. Who's it going to hurt?"

"But Val is not a lesbian," Greg countered. "She should not encourage the little dyke."

Valerie shot back angrily, "That kid is barely a teenager. Do you think she knows what a dyke is, Greg?"

"I just think someone should set her straight, that's all. She should know it isn't normal."

Margie was shocked when Val said, "Who are you to decide what is normal?"

"Look," Greg began, "I know it's normal for girls to crush on each other, but that has to be nipped in the bud before it stunts healthy sexual desires."

"I suppose the boys' circle jerks are just part of a healthy maturation process."

Margie tried not to laugh at Val's response. She kept her eyes on the swimmers squeezing the last seconds out of open swim time.

"Do whatever you want, Val," Greg said, as he turned to go. "I just think it is a mistake."

Val turned her attention to Margie. "I think it's kind of sweet that the kid wants to show me her sailing skills."

"She's good," Margie said. "Maybe it will be fun. Her heart will pitter-patter, and she'll have a camp story to relive."

"Your empathy sounds authentic," Val said, as she came close enough to make Margie's heart do a patter of its own.

Val blew the whistle, ending swim time and Margie's predicament. While securing the swimming area equipment and shutting down for the night, she saw Val approach Greg at the boat dock, with the little skipper in tow. By the time Margie clipped the rope across the entrance, which was really no more than a strong suggestion that the swimming area was closed for the evening, Val and the skipper were sailing away.

Margie followed their progress from the shoreline, admiring the skill with which the sunfish crisscrossed the river. Margie was an experienced sailor too. She had taken a boat out just this morning. While making a long run toward the flats that opened out to the Atlantic, she noticed the oyster bar was barely visible just under the surface. She narrowly avoided a nasty crash. As she trailed behind Val, wondering if she might be the stalker instead of the kid at the helm, Margie realized the sunfish was headed toward the bar. That's when she had begun running.

"Hey, Val. The oyster bar. Watch out for the bar!" Margie yelled as she ran toward the end of the pier.

Her effort was in vain. She arrived in time to see the centerboard catch the bar and rocket up between Val's outstretched legs. The sudden stop sent Val sliding crotch first into a violent collision with the solid oak centerboard.

"That is going to hurt," Margie said to herself.

She turned toward the mess hall. A bag of ice was going to be Val's friend for a reasonably long recovery period.

#

When Margie arrived at the boat dock, Val was sitting on the back of the sunfish, apparently trying to decide if she could walk and if so, should she? The young captain, who was already distraught over injuring the one person she wished to impress with her sailing skills, became flustered during a painful apology, let go of the wrong rope, and dropped the boom on Val's head. That was all the kid could take. She abandoned all hope of regaining any dignity and took off running. Margie thought it was best to let her go and see to Val's injuries.

"Are you okay, Val," Margie asked.

Val had one hand in her crotch and the other on the top of her head. She began to shake, which worried Margie until she realized the injured Val was laughing.

"Oh, my God," Val said. "That little lesbian tried to kill me."

"Man, I'm glad you're laughing," Margie said, laughing too. "I'm also glad she took off like that. Had she stayed around, she might have done some real damage." She held out the bag of ice to Val. "Here, you can decide which bruise hurts the most."

"Val, are you okay?" Greg asked as he ran up. "Where's that kid? I'm going to put a stop to this bull shit."

"Oh, stop, Greg. She's just an embarrassed kid." Val stood up, gingerly. "Woo. Maybe that wasn't a good idea."

Margie stepped forward to support Val. "Whoa, there," she said, as she wrapped an arm around Val's waist. "Let's go see the nurse and get you checked out."

"Who's going to de-rig and store this boat?" Greg asked.

"That's your job," Val said. "Come on, Margie. I think I'm going to need more ice and some whiskey to put it in."

#

The nurse gave Val a Darvocet and sent her to bed, where it was recommended she not to be left alone. The head injury was a glancing blow, but her crotch was going to hurt for a few days.

"You're going to want to ice that area down every few hours," the nurse said. "That's going to be a hell of a pelvic bruise, but your important bits are unharmed."

When the head lifeguard left, Val inherited her job and the one tiny private cabin on the female side of the grounds. Greg showed up just as Margie was delivering the patient to her digs.

Greg dismissed Margie. "Thank you for taking care of her," he said, as he slid his hand under Val's elbow and moved her away, though she didn't need the steadying.

"She isn't supposed to be alone," Margie explained.

"It's okay. She won't be," Greg answered.

"But after curfew, who will be here then," Margie asked, immediately regretting the naiveté.

Val, sounding a bit loopy, giggled. "Oh, my God, Margie. You're so funny."

Greg said, "Hey, would you mind bringing some chow, when you come back this way," as he led Val into her cabin. He smirked as he passed Margie. "Be sure to knock first."

#

About two hours later, Margie approached Val's cabin balancing a tray of burgers, fries, and two ice teas from the mess hall. She didn't mind bringing Val something to eat, but she hoped Greg choked on it. With about thirty feet left to reach the door of the cabin, it flew open and out rushed Greg. He didn't see Margie. He rounded the corner and disappeared from sight.

She heard him say, "Hey, you! Stop right there."

Margie carefully placed the tray on the cabin steps and followed Greg around the side.

"I just wanted to say I was sorry," the skillful skipper said, nearly in tears.

Greg wagged a finger in the young girl's face. "You've done enough damage. Stay away from her for the rest of the week. Do you hear me?"

"I didn't do it on purpose," the kid said.

"Your fascination isn't normal. Knock it off."

The kid's face went ashen. She looked like she was going to puke.

Margie, who had until that moment lacked the courage to interfere, took two long strides and stepped between the girl and her menace.

"Hey, Greg. You know what isn't normal? A twenty-year-old who is so insecure he has to attack a young girl obviously in need of comfort, not chastisement."

"Well, one dyke taking up for another. How perfectly predictable."

"Fuck off, Greg."

Margie turned to see Val, who had apparently heard plenty.

"Go back inside, Val. Let me deal with these two. If you had let me nip this little one's infatuation in the bud, you wouldn't be recovering from a bruised pussy."

"Wow. You really are a piece of shit, aren't you?" Val came closer and took the young girl's hand. "Come with me, darling. Greg was just leaving, and Margie is going to walk you back to your cabin."

"Fine!" Greg stomped away.

"Thank you, Miss Val. I'm really sorry about the boat ride and everything." The kid was crushed.

Margie smiled when Val leaned down and kissed the girl on the forehead. "It's okay, hon'. Accidents happen. I enjoyed the ride, right up to the part when I didn't." She laughed.

The kid laughed.

Margie fell in love.

#

Margie knocked on the cabin door. She had delivered the young girl to her chaperone and returned as Val requested. Margie was elated when, by process of elimination, telling Greg to "Fuck off," she had been given the job of watching Val sleep.

"Come in," came the invitation.

"Best of My Love," played on the radio as Margie entered.

Val took two steps across the room, tangled a hand in the back of Margie's hair, and stilled her lips a heart-stopping fraction away from fulfilling a fantasy.

"I thought you might want to help me ice down," Val whispered. She brushed her lips against Margie's and asked, "Have you ever kissed a girl before?"

Margie smiled. "A few."

"I had a suspicion that might be the case," Val said.

She pushed Margie against the wall and pressed her body against her.

"How about you?" Margie asked. "How many girls have you kissed?"

"Just one. A night of drinking among friends. I don't remember much."

"Really? I would have never guessed, the way you grabbed my hair and your close proximity to my lips at the moment."

"I've wanted to do this and a few other things since the first time I saw you."

"What about your injuries?"

"I don't know, I think we can work around that. We have plenty of ice, should we need it."

"What about Greg?"

"Stop stalling and kiss me, Margie Whooten."

Margie closed the distance between their lips too fast to let Val change her mind.

#

On August 16, 1977, Elvis Presley, the King of Rock and Roll dies in his home, Graceland, at the age of forty-two. 75,000 fans line the streets of Memphis for his funeral held on August 18th. The King is dead. Long live the King.

#

August 21, 1977

Dear Ruth Ann,

You are never going to believe what happened. You were right. Keeping my options open has led to some amazing opportunities. It all started when Ida and Bob decided I needed to go work at a summer camp...

About the author…

Four-time Lambda Literary Award Finalist in Mystery—*Rainey Nights* (2012), *Molly: House on Fire* (2013), *The Rainey Season* (2014), and *Relatively Rainey* (2016)—and 2013 Rainbow Awards First Runner-up for Best Lesbian Novel, *Out on the Panhandle*, author R. E. Bradshaw began publishing in August of 2010. Before beginning a full-time writing career, she worked in professional theatre and also taught at both university and high school levels. A native of North Carolina, the setting for the majority of her novels, Bradshaw now makes her home in Oklahoma. Writing in many genres, from the fun southern romantic romps of the Adventures of Decky and Charlie series to the intensely bone-chilling Rainey Bell Thrillers, R. E. Bradshaw's books offer something for everyone.

www.ingramcontent.com/pod-product-compliance
Lightning Source LLC
Chambersburg PA
CBHW052142220626
47052CB00005B/1156